# A Deadly Deception

ANGUS BRODIE AND MIKAELA FORSYTHE MURDER
MYSTERY
BOOK SEVEN

## CARLA SIMPSON

OLIVERHEBERBOOKS

## Prologue

THE SHADES at the window were hastily lowered. Then a light glowed in the room.

It gleamed off glass jars, the steel surface of the table, the chair, and the surgical instruments on a steel tray.

"It is too soon. I told you... you must give the incisions time to heal."

"Four weeks! It has been long enough!" Then, "You have been well paid for your time and your expertise."

"I cannot guarantee there won't be repercussions..."

He cut him off. "I have not paid you for guarantees. Only results. Now, get on with it, and I will be on my way."

"You must continue to rest. To do this now might well ruin everything."

"I do not need your advice, only that you finish this now."

It began, slowly, carefully, each bandage loosened then removed. One by one, discarded.

Then another bandage removed as the face of the man in the chair gradually emerged. Another bandage just below the eyes was peeled away and revealed high cheekbones and a patrician nose.

One more, the hand that held the bandage trembling, as full lips were revealed, and curved in a smile after the weeks of waiting, and the chiseled chin beneath with a sparse growth of beard upon the barely healed skin.

Six weeks he'd waited... Longer, truth be known.

The search, the risk, and the deception was close at hand.

"Mirror!" he demanded as the last bandage was removed.

It was thrust into his hand and he stared at the reflection, the arch of the brows, the nose, cheeks with only thin scars remaining at the hairline.

He slowly smiled, testing the feel of it, the look of it. Perfect.

For weeks he'd waited, planned, fought his way through the pain, paced the flat where he'd hidden himself away, going out only at night to come here so that the bandages could be changed.

A genius, he was told of the man he'd found. A man who could work miracles. And he had.

Only one thing remained to be done, he thought, as he grabbed the man by the front of the surgeon's coat, seized the knife from the steel tray and plunged it into the man's throat.

The surgeon flailed, a stunned expression on his face, blood spurting from the wound as he stared at his creation.

Newly shaped lips curved in a smile as he slowly lowered him to the floor.

The surgeon wouldn't be found right away, in this secret place where he worked his little miracles. But it didn't matter.

There were no records, no names written anywhere. He had seen to it with each payment that bought the surgeon's skill and his silence for the experimental procedure.

What was one more death, when the most important one waited?

He seized the bandages and threw them in the coal stove, then slipped on the pristine white shirt from the exclusive tailor's shop. The only blood was in a pool surrounding the good doctor.

Then he scattered the other instruments, threw the jars to the floor, and tore books from the shelves— including the book he'd read about the procedure, as old as the Egyptians.

When he was finished it looked as if there had been a robbery, the physician murdered in the midst of it. Not uncommon in that part of London.

He donned the cravat then his long coat and hat, taking care with the freshly healed skin on each side of his head and neck.

Then, out the door, the misty night air redolent with the stench that was almost constant in London, the sliver of dawn at the embankment.

After months, countless meetings, planning, and the painful surgeries and recovery that had followed, it was finally time to set their plan in motion...

# *One*

DECEMBER, 1890, LONDON

OUR COACH PULLED in through the gated entrance at Sussex Square, my great-aunt's residence in London.

Lady Antonia Montgomery, my great-aunt, had raised my sister and me after the deaths of both our parents. She was the nearest family there was for the both of us.

Except of course for the man seated across from me, Angus Brodie, formerly of the Metropolitan Police now with his own private inquiry business, and... under circumstances that were still quite surprising for me— my husband. At least as far as the magistrate in the north of Scotland was satisfied.

I say, quite surprising, as I had been fairly certain, until two years ago, precisely what the path of my life would be. I had avoided that dreaded state of matrimony with particular expectations for one of my station.

I had previously ended what I was certain was going to be a very boring and mind-numbing proper betrothal, and begun my travels that included Europe, the Near East, encountered the Bedouin, sailed the Nile, and lived for some time in the Far

East where I had followed my curiosity and experienced things that respectable English women simply did not do.

That included dueling lessons in France— I was quite accomplished in that, the ancient art of self-defense in the Orient, and other sports while proper ladies indulged in games of whist or lawn tennis, and quietly discussed when they might be given the vote after it was banned some decades earlier.

It might be said that my unusual childhood, raised in the wilds of Scotland at my aunt's estate, Old Lodge, or her somewhat unconventional household in London, might not have been the proper environment for two young girls.

It might be... But I had loved it and as for my sister, she had survived quite nicely.

Now it seemed that earlier experience with my aunt had come full circle. Or possibly a partial circle in the young girl who was now my ward.

It was one of those occasions where I had leapt before I looked, so to speak, after encountering Lily in a previous inquiry case in Edinburgh.

She was orphaned as far as she or anyone knew, working in a brothel... No, not that sort of work. She was the women's maid and worldly beyond her years, with a fiery disposition and courage that I much admired.

She had been helpful in assisting me during the case, even at the risk to herself. Admittedly, she had seen it as a great adventure in her otherwise dull and boring life.

The thought of her returning to work in a brothel or tavern which I had seen far too many times in the East End, was not something I was willing to accept.

I had made a proposal to provide for her education and care for the next several years. Perhaps more than a little suspicious of my offer— something I could identify with —she had initially refused.

Then I had received a telegram informing me that she had changed her mind. Mr. Munro, the manager of my aunt's estates, had set off to Edinburgh to retrieve her. She had arrived very nearly two months before, wide-eyed, curious yet guarded, and declared that she would give it a try.

It was pointed out at the time by more than one person, including Brodie, that she reminded them of me. I do not know where that idea came from.

It might have been that hint of stubbornness, determination to do things her own way, and that insatiable curiosity.

Whatever the reason, here we were.

Lily spent a great deal of time at Sussex Square for a variety of reasons, which my aunt had immediately pointed out.

Reason number one: Our aunt had previous experience as a parental figure with my sister and I, and she was quite accustomed to having someone young about.

Reason number two: My aunt knew precisely the best people to contact. That included tutors, dressmakers, and most particularly someone who was well-schooled in proper elocution.

Lily, my aunt declared, could simply not go about speaking as she did when she first arrived. She would either find herself in a brawl or the gaol. There was that influence of the streets and the brothel, which I fully understood.

Admittedly she had a habit of cursing, quite colorful with that Scots accent. I thought the person in charge of that might have their hands full as I was still given to a colorful word myself from time to time.

Reason number three: There were my novels and the cases I participated in with Brodie, along with that other situation...

A newly married woman needed to spend time with her husband, my aunt declared. However, not from practical experience it should be noted.

At the age of almost eighty-five years she had never wed. Not for lack of interest or suitors, but simply for lack of anyone who fit into her life. And there was that strong-willed, independent nature.

I had wondered where mine came from. I didn't need to look any further than my aunt.

The apple, as they say, had not fallen far from that tree, a tree that went back to the time of William the Conqueror with an assortment of noblemen and thieves along the way.

I, too, had declared that I would never wed...

Then, there was Brodie.

He could be stubborn, from the streets as they say, not at all the sort of man a proper young woman might choose. But despite his rough edges and curses when he was angry, his loyalty went soul deep. He was also the most honorable man I had ever met, I thought, looking across at him now.

And he was devilishly handsome with those dark eyes that looked at me in a certain way... when he wasn't angry with me over something. That certain way reminded me of our very first unexpected encounter some years before, then again when he had helped in the matter of finding my sister in that first inquiry case.

Then there was that other thing...

It was something my aunt, of all people, had told me. He made my toes curl... with just that look in those dark eyes, and what usually followed.

So, there it was, all of my well-intentioned plans out the window so to speak— married, very well married, thank you, even though there were still parts of this that Brodie and I were still figuring out; much like a murder case to be investigated.

And there was the role of parent, that seemed very much to be an arrangement with the whole family, including my sister who had recently declared that Lily's manners were atrocious, and was determined that she needed some refinement. That included music and voice lessons.

I thought that might be taking things a bit far, but had decided to withhold any judgment in that regard. Lily certainly didn't seem the refined, musical sort. But then what did I know about raising a half-grown young woman, other than having once been one.

For all those reasons, Lily spent a great deal of time at Sussex Square. She had my old room, and the sword room— a girl after my own heart on that.

For his part, Brodie had not hesitated at the arrangement. He had merely cautioned that she was not a child, but a young woman very nearly grown, who had the sort of life experiences that others had not.

But the truth was, that so far he made a wonderful father figure— stern when he had to be, indulgent in ways he never had experienced as a child himself, and supportive of me— while juggling inquiry cases and new work for the Agency.

As for today, my sister, Lenore, had sent round a message that Lily was to give a music recital for the family this afternoon.

So here we were, Brodie and I, navigating this new aspect of our relationship, and attending Lily's first recital.

Upon our arrival and greeting by my aunt's head butler, Mr. Symons, we discovered that a "small family affair" included several of my aunt's close acquaintances, those she usually invited for cards or tarot readings.

My sister, Linnie, met us at the entrance to the grand salon.

"Mikaela, Mr. Brodie, I am so glad that you're here," she greeted us. "Lily has been doing marvelous with her lessons and I thought this would be a way of rewarding her."

I wasn't certain about the reward part of that comment. The day before Lily had taken me aside and asked if there was something else she might do besides the "stinkin' music lessons."

"What am I supposed to do with music lessons?" she had asked.

She most certainly wasn't shy expressing an opinion.

It seemed that Linnie's opinions of Lily's enthusiasm for music and voice lessons might be a bit different than hers. And given her outright dislike, I didn't bother to mention that refined skills such as music were often expected of a young woman in anticipation of marriage.

"I'm a-feared that I'll go mush-headed with all the music, and voice lessons," Lily had bemoaned, reminiscent of myself at her age.

"It's boring!"

At her age, I had tried and succeeded at doing anything other than those boring lessons myself, which accounted for the fact that I much preferred music hall or stage performances by my friend, Templeton, over operas and concerts.

I had persuaded Lily to keep up with the lessons a little longer and here we were. She had been encouraged that it might only be for a little while longer, however looking over at her now seated at the piano, she looked absolutely miserable.

"Mr. Adams says that she does show promise," Linnie continued, as we gave our coats and umbrellas to Mr. Symons.

Promise?

I exchanged a look with Brodie. He refused to respond to my sister on that one and I was inclined to agree.

I glanced about the music room, then at Lily.

My aunt rose from her chair and swept across the floor toward us.

"This is so exciting," she declared. "Mr. Adams has high hopes for her. He said that Lily is quite talented."

I was already aware of that, however my aunt's definition of talented did not include escaping a burning building, picking pockets, or a vocabulary of curses that would have made the most common street person envious.

Brodie and I were working on that one with her. However, there was a saying that you couldn't make a silk purse out of a sow's ear. While I did not consider Lily to be the latter, I was convinced that she had no use for the silk purse part of it. At least not the part that included music and voice lessons. Bravo, I thought.

"This should be most interestin'," Brodie commented as he escorted me across the salon to our chairs.

I was to remember that, along with a dozen more things afterward, in what followed.

Mr. Adams had Lily start with a piece from Beethoven that I recognized, then a piece I was not familiar with— in consideration of my own rebellion at her age.

"Mozart," my sister whispered. "I've always loved this piece, and she is quite good, don't you think?"

Quite bored, came to mind as I watched her fingers fly across the keys, her mouth thinned.

While I thought her efforts quite exemplary, I saw the explosion coming.

"Oh, dear," I whispered.

"What is it?" Brodie replied.

There was no time to explain, only the sound as Lily's hands pounced on the piano keys.

Pounced was certainly the right word. She then launched into a different piece, complete with colorful lyrics.

*"There was a girl from Halifax who went about in her garters; She charged six pence for just a look, and more to share her quarters..."*

I thought the esteemed Mr. Adams might have apoplexy, as Lily then moved on to another equally colorful verse.

Brodie made a sound, his hand over his mouth— he might have been clearing his throat. However, I could have sworn there was a smile there, that dark gaze meeting mine.

"A tune you're familiar with?" I whispered as Mr. Adams attempted to end the recital.

"I havena heard it in a while."

"From your time as a boy on the streets of Edinburgh?" I asked with equal amusement.

I glanced over at Lily. I could have sworn there was a triumphant smile in that dark gaze with that glint of blue about the edges that I had seen before during that inquiry case in Edinburgh.

All the while she pounded the keys of the piano, in spite of Mr. Adams' best efforts to encourage her back to Mozart, and swung into a bawdy chorus— that was the only word for it — her dark hair dancing about her shoulders.

"There is another part of it she hasna gotten to yet," he commented, then cautioned. "Ye might want to intervene before one of her ladyship's acquaintances faints from the experience."

Good advice, I thought. I rose and crossed the salon. I laid a hand on Lily's shoulder.

"Most entertaining," I complimented her, struggling to keep the laughter from my voice.

"Do ye like it, miss? There's more to it," she replied.

According to Brodie there was a great deal more to it, however with a glance about the salon I wasn't at all certain that the others would survive it.

Except for my aunt, of course, who struggled with her own amusement. As for my sister, she had closed her eyes and simply shook her head.

"I think refreshments are in order," my aunt announced as Mr. Adams attempted to apologize to her for Lily's lack of "proficiency."

"Proficiency?" my aunt exclaimed. "It would seem that she was most proficient."

I suspected that was completely lost on Mr. Adams who considered himself quite the master of music. He hadn't a clue, unlike my aunt and myself, that Lily had achieved exactly what she had intended. And it was an amusing little ditty, I had to admit. The sort that one cannot forget and keeps playing over and over in one's head.

Refreshments were served that included tea and scones. I wasn't one for tea, but the scones were wonderful.

Lily had not yet adjusted to the fact that there was more than enough food at my townhouse in Mayfair, or here at Sussex Square. I caught her slipping two scones into the pocket of her gown.

She looked up at me with unabashed bravado. "Fer later tonight. I might get hungry." She glanced past me. "There's no harm is there, Mr. Brodie?"

That earlier bemused expression was gone, replaced by a slight frown surrounded by that dark beard.

"No harm," he assured her, as he leaned in close, and I caught the faint scent of cinnamon about him that I so enjoyed.

"I must be going," he informed me.

I didn't bother to hide my disappointment. I was expected at a reception within the hour and had hoped he might accompany me. And afterward...

"Sir Avery?" I replied.

"Aye, some important work that I need to attend to."

It was not my habit to be petulant or unreasonable about things. I usually went my own way as was my habit. Still there was disappointment. It was one of those things we were still trying to figure out about this new aspect of our relationship, along with a myriad of others.

"Work?" Lily exclaimed. "What sort of work?"

That was another one of the things. Lily knew about our inquiry cases, but she wasn't aware of his work for the Agency and had only recently learned of my other vocation as it were— as an author.

Brodie didn't offer Lily an explanation now, as he obviously thought it best to keep that aspect of his work between the two of us.

He slipped a finger beneath my chin, drawing my attention. It was a rare public gesture as he was surprisingly quite reserved about that sort of thing in public. Imagine that, Brodie shy about something. The gestures in private however, more than made up for it.

"I know that ye have that reception this afternoon," he said then. "I will try to be there."

"Of course."

This was not the first time we would need to go our separate ways, and undoubtedly would not be the last. Our inquiry cases had a way of taking precedence.

That brought up the question, what sort of work was he involved in that he had so far chosen not to share with me?

"Reception?" Lily asked.

I explained as my aunt's driver brought the coach round.

"And they throw a party when ye have a new book?" she exclaimed.

I replied that it was all a part of getting my name out there... or rather that of Emma Fortescue and promoting each new book as it was released by the publisher.

"Now," I said as we settled in the coach. "You must tell me about the performance you gave. It was most interesting."

That dark blue gaze met mine. "Ye're not angry with me, are ye?"

I loved her lively spirit and stubbornness about things. Those qualities had most certainly saved both of our lives in that previous case in Scotland. She was brave and self-confident. Most of the time.

Her question now revealed another side that was hesitant, perhaps vulnerable, and I reminded myself that in making the decision to take me up on my offer and come to London, she was taking an enormous chance with people she hardly knew.

And I loved her impromptu performance.

I smiled, remembering some of my own transgressions very near her age.

"I loved it," I told her. "You must perform all of it some time."

"And her ladyship?" she asked with a noticeable quiver in her voice which told me a great deal as well.

"Trust me, she loved it as well."

I then shared what was considered a transgression of mine when I was unable to tolerate another boring lesson. It had to do with escaping the second-floor room at Sussex Square in nothing more than my camisole and knickers before one of our tutors arrived.

That particular episode precluded my aunt's decision to send my sister and I to private school in France.

"France?" Lily exclaimed. "I've heard wicked things about France. However did ye survive?"

"Quite well actually." For now, I did not go into further details.

That would be a conversation for another day.

*Two*

LILY AND I arrived at Hatchards book shop at Number 187 Piccadilly in good time. I had my aunt's driver let us off just across the way and we crossed the street.

There were several people, mostly ladies and a handful of men, in a queue that reached from the shop out to the sidewalk.

And there in the window case my latest book was on display along with a placard that announced the reception for that afternoon.

*"Did you read her last book?"* a young woman who might have been near my own age commented.

*"Absolutely wonderful! Her heroine, Emma Fortescue, is now investigating murder! And she is absolutely fearless! Now, there is a woman after my own heart!"*

*"Most interesting. The author is actually a noblewoman. I hear that she's gone off on those very same adventures..."*

*"I read in the dailies that she assisted in the solving of a murder with a private investigator..."*

*"I do hope that she will be here..."*

There were several other comments, not all of them flattering.

*"My sister sent me to purchase her latest book,"* a man then added. *"I wouldn't be caught dead reading anything by a woman!"*

*"Your sister?"* another young woman replied. *"Of course, if it makes you happy to say that. However, most men might learn something about how to treat an independent woman by reading it!"*

Lily looked up at me with a surprised expression. "Men read yer books as well?"

I maneuvered our way past the line. "So it seems."

Of course I appreciated the accolades, along with the somewhat veiled criticism.

I had put a great deal of time and effort into each book, developing my heroine, Emma Fortescue, along the way. She was most amusing.

*"Good heavens!"* my sister had commented when she read my first book. *"Did you really do all those things?"*

As for our aunt. *"I've always wanted to do that. Do you think I still have time at my age?"*

My answer in both instances was— Yes, of course!

I made my way to the table at the back of the shop where several of my books awaited my signature.

My publisher, Mr. Warren, and the owner of the shop had agreed that a personal appearance along with signed copies of my book had a way of bringing people inside, rather than perusing the display at the window and then walking past. Something on the order of a curiosity.

The owner had also arranged to serve afternoon tea in the back of the shop in an area that had been created to resemble a parlor in a private residence.

Lily picked up one of my books. "You wrote this?" she exclaimed as she slowly read my name.

"I might be able to read it real soon. Her ladyship says that I'm verra quick with my lessons."

That could be most interesting, I thought, as Mr. Warren joined us.

I introduced Lily to him.

"Ye're the one Miss Lenore is keeping company with," she replied.

I did hope she hadn't just insulted Mr. Warren. He looked over at me with some amusement.

"I suppose the answer would be yes," he replied.

Lily, smart as a whip, quickly came to both our rescue.

"That's it," she explained. "She said as how you was a right smart-lookin' sort."

Of course that was in comparison with some of the customers Lily might have encountered at the brothel in Edinburgh. Never let it be said that she didn't say exactly what she was thinking.

My aunt was working on her social skills as well as her education, however Lily's lapse in manners was a word of warning to me. Although I found her blunt honesty somewhat reminiscent of my own outspokenness.

I gave Mr. Warren a sympathetic smile. "Lily has recently come to London and is presently staying with my aunt. Lenore is assisting with art lessons."

"I do believe she mentioned something about that," he commented. "Most admirable of yourself and Lady Montgomery. Perhaps a subject for a future book?" he suggested.

I could only imagine what that might include.

"We are to attend a gallery showing this evening. Two of

your sister's paintings will be on display," he continued. "I'm quite excited for her. Did she pass along any note, perhaps?"

She hadn't. But then she had been fully involved with the recital and then the aftermath of Lily's *unexpected* performance.

"She's waited for this for a long time," I replied and assured him. "I'm so very glad that you support her in this."

"Of course!" he enthusiastically replied. "And she is so very talented. Artistic talent seems to run in the family."

I did like Mr. Warren very much and hoped that my sister didn't send him off as she had other men following the demise of her marriage. And that was the only word for it— demise, as in death!

"Come along then," he said, taking our coats. "You have the table, just there. I've had a pen set out so that you may sign the books along with any comment you wish to add. We have found that readers do like the personal touch, as if they are part of... your adventures.

"If you are asked when your next book will be available," he continued, "we have scheduled it for May of the coming year. And of course, they may also purchase previous books and follow Miss Emma Fortescue's other adventures."

I thanked him for meeting me at the shop. I was aware that not all publishers made that gesture. Certainly not my first publisher, who had called my first two books, *"Outlandish accounts of a wayward young woman."*

I learned they had been published as a "favor" to my aunt. I had then met Mr. Warren, who was very near Brodie's age and without the usual bias against books written by a woman. Most particularly adventure books about a young woman who *"flaunted the usual conventions of society,"* as one critic— obviously a man —had commented in the dailies.

Mr. Warren had embraced the books and Emma Fortescue as a well-educated, modern young woman, and those who read them as, *"quenching a thirst for departure from the same roles of their mothers before them, before they were allowed to wear split walking skirts, ride bicycles, and partake in sports."*

My books had become surprisingly successful. They were read wrapped inside the daily newspaper, discussed at ladies' club meetings, and had resulted in an invitation for me to speak to the Ladies Auxiliary League regarding women's rights.

I had declined at the time, as I was quite involved in solving a murder case with Brodie. And there was that other part of my response that I hadn't mentioned. I preferred the anonymity of the pen name that allowed me to come and go about as needed in my work with Brodie.

It was Brodie, quite surprisingly, who suggested that I accept Mr. Warren's proposal for readers to meet with the author— namely myself. In addition, he had been most encouraging of the time I was spending on the next book— during a time that he was increasingly well occupied at the Agency.

I frowned. It seemed he was far too occupied with the Agency of late, particularly since our return from Scotland. And he had been quite secretive about it.

"I'm very excited for this latest book," Mr. Warren now commented. "I do believe people, including men, will find it exciting." He nodded toward the line of patrons that did indeed contain at least two men.

I had taken a chair at the table while Lily had taken herself off to explore the bookstore.

"Imagine people writing all these books," she had exclaimed. "And people actually read them!"

"Good heavens, but she is refreshing," Mr. Warren

commented with genuine enthusiasm. "Perhaps a companion for Miss Emma Fortescue's future adventures?"

"Good heavens" might be polite understatement, I thought, as I watched her pull a book from a nearby shelf, her nose wrinkling as she attempted to read it.

I smiled as I recognized that particular book by Jane Austen. A good place to start, I thought, then move on to Emma Fortescue.

"The manager of the shop has more than enough copies of your book," Mr. Warren was saying, "and the earlier ones as well for new readers." Then he added, "Thank you for agreeing to be here. I do believe that it will be most exciting for your readers."

He turned to leave, with a smile for those waiting. "Thank you again, *Emma Fortescue,*" he said in parting.

I had no idea how many people, if any, might attend the afternoon tea and book signing event and had braced myself for those who might make disparaging comments. I had encountered those before. Mr. Warren had cautioned that the books came with a certain *notoriety,* as he put it.

I hadn't written that first book, the second one, or even the more recent ones with that in mind. I had simply written them about a young Englishwoman's adventures as she traveled to foreign places.

The notoriety they created had come later as women, according to my sister, could be found secretly reading them. My friend, Templeton, somewhat notorious herself, would love that.

Breaking down barriers, Mr. Warren had called it, often put those breaking them on the firing line, so to speak. There were always those who were critical simply to be critical, or those who were either frightened or resistant to change.

Onward, I thought as the first of the shop's customers stepped up to the table. A woman, very near my aunt's age. She smiled sweetly.

"I've read all your Emma books," she said with a giggle. She handed me the latest one to sign the inside page.

"I've heard that she resembles yourself perhaps?"

"Perhaps," I replied.

"How I would have loved to do as she has," she said as I finished signing. "I suppose that I'm too old now."

"I know someone very near eighty-five years old," I confided. "She is planning on going on safari to Africa."

"Oh, how wonderful," she said with a twinkle in her eye. "Or possibly the Greek Islands?" she suggested.

"The water is incredible," I replied as I handed the book back to her.

"Greek Islands?" Lily asked as she returned from her wanderings about the shop. "I've heard of them from one of the ladies in Edinburgh. She said that's where men keep company with men." She wrinkled her nose in that way I was quickly beginning to realize accompanied something she either didn't understand or didn't like.

"Well, not according to my own experience," I replied.

"What about Mr. Brodie?" she asked as I took the book from the next lady and opened it to sign.

Oh, yes. What about Mr. Brodie?

"That was before I knew him," I explained.

The nose wrinkle was still there. "I canna imagine he would approve of that."

I didn't bother to explain the rest of it, that he had in fact been there although it wasn't something I had remembered at the time. There was a great deal of ouzo involved. When in Greece...

Brodie had been quite assertive when it came to finding, then retrieving, a young woman whose aunt had sent him to find her after receiving several communications from other travelers about her behavior. But that was also a conversation for another day.

Tea was served for those who wished to stay at the shop for a while and explore other books available. It was a mix of young women, very near my own age when I first began my adventures, some older women such as the woman who was concerned about her age and the possibility of her own adventures.

An older man, quite scholarly, approached the table. A student had suggested my books as opposed to the *"boring"* texts that were required reading in his class.

"Not precisely on the same level with Greek or Roman studies of my students," he quipped. He clearly considered my books beneath him.

"Have you read one of my other books?" I asked, quite curious at his statement.

"Not as yet," he admitted.

"Ah," I replied, then added in Latin, "*non potest iudicare quod quis non legit.*" *One cannot judge what one has not read.* Admittedly, I was not familiar with the Greek version of that particular bit of wisdom.

"Quite so," he replied with more than a little surprise as I handed the book back to him.

"I look forward to reading it," he admitted with a bit of bemused curiosity.

"I look forward to your reading it," I replied.

Another man who had been waiting in line, looked very much like a bookkeeper or possibly a librarian, somewhat nervous I thought, surrounded by several women. He shifted the glasses he wore and smiled hesitantly.

"This is for my wife," he explained, pushing the glasses back up his nose again. "She has read your other books."

I asked her name, then signed the book. *"For Jane, thank you. Emma Fortescue."*

I had long adopted the habit of signing as my other self. It avoided confusion, even though there were those who knew that Emma Fortescue was purely a fictionalized person.

I shared tea and biscuits with Lily and customers who lingered. I answered questions and shared small bits of other adventures with them, as the manager of Hatchards brought out more books for people to purchase.

"Miss Emma Fortescue, I presume?"

The voice was articulate, educated in that way of those who attended Harrow or Eton, but with a faint shadow of some other accent, possibly from having traveled abroad. It had a way of slipping into one's speech after a time.

"Or should I say, Lady Forsythe?"

There was recognition on the gentleman's part. Mine came somewhat more slowly.

"I realize that it has been some time," he added. "Cairo and the pyramids beyond for several weeks," he said then as I hesitated.

"Admittedly, I am a bit older now," he continued. "However are you unchanged? And, obviously quite successful," he added with a glance about the crowded shop.

"And, if I may say so, quite extraordinary as well. You were never shy, as I remember. A young woman traveling alone cannot be that. But you have changed in the intervening time." He reached out and took my hand.

"And most excellently, I must say."

"Sir James Redstone," I replied, as the memory came back.

"It has been almost eight years since Egypt," he admitted. "And as I recall, your first adventure abroad."

"I believe it was almost ten years ago," I replied.

He smiled then, "However, a pleasure to see you again. I have only just returned from abroad and learned of this event." He glanced about the shop.

"You seem to have done quite well for yourself," he complimented. "Your second novel?"

"It's her sixth novel," Lily boldly corrected him.

"And who might this young lady be?" he asked with what appeared to be amusement.

Not to be set aside, Lily replied, "Miss Mikaela and Mr. Brodie's ward."

Admittedly her manners needed to be polished, however there was a noticeable sharpness in her answer. I introduced her to Sir James.

"That must have been a bad injury," she added looking at his other hand.

I had noticed the absence of his ring finger and the smaller one next to it, a new injury obviously more recent since our last acquaintance.

"Must make it difficult to lift a pint."

For the sake of propriety and to avoid any further comments, I suggested that she find Mr. Warren and inquire about additional books that he had mentioned.

There was definitely a mischievous glint in those blue eyes.

"Of course, miss."

"Your ward?" he replied.

Again that faint curiosity was there. I wasn't at all certain whether it was for Lily's impudence, or the fact that I was now in charge of a young person very near the age when Sir James and I first met.

"We're assisting her with her education, and…"

"Manners?" he suggested.

"She can be rather outspoken," I admitted. "My apologies."

"Most charming, and nothing to apologize for, Mikaela."

Charming was not a word I would have used.

"You have recently returned from your latest travels," I maneuvered the conversation in another direction.

"Yes," he replied. "I have just returned from Alexandria. Fascinating place, Egypt, I am certain you well remember."

The conversation continued in that direction, recalling some of the places we had both visited on that journey that had been quite eye-opening for myself, having never before ventured farther than Paris or my aunt's estate in the south of France.

I remembered our first encounter and the fact that I had been quite taken with Sir James and his vast knowledge of some of the places we visited on my first adventure.

He seemed much the same now, aristocratic bearing, quite tall, with perfectly groomed dark brown hair. That blue gaze that I had once found to be quite mesmerizing, with lean, handsome features seemed hardly changed.

"You would be quite interested in the recent antiquities that were brought out of Luxor," he was saying now. "I also had the opportunity to spend time at the Temple of Edfu. Most fascinating. Of course, there are many travelers that visit now."

I remembered that trip down the Nile, recommended to me by a friend of my aunt, Amelia Edwards, who had first whetted my appetite for adventure. A noted journalist and adventurer, herself, she had recently returned from what she called her last visit to that ancient land.

She was very near my aunt's age, but time and those countless foreign explorations had taken a toll. However, even with white in her hair, there was still that glint of curiosity in her eyes.

*"It's the misery in my knees,"* she had explained on that last visit I had made. *"I fear that I have ventured through the pyramids and tombs for the last time."* She winked at me then. *"Now it is time to write about my adventures."*

I noticed the glazed expression now in Lily's eyes. Boredom, I thought. Or possibly something else?

"And what of yourself?" Sir James then inquired. "Obviously you have found success with your novels... Five of them now, I stand corrected."

This was said with a glance at Lily, who looked at him with that same faintly bored expression. Definitely something else behind her dark blue gaze that usually had such a lively expression.

The shop manager approached to thank me for appearing that afternoon as the last of the customers departed and I realized it was very near the closing hour. He was greatly pleased with the number of book sales that afternoon.

"If you would be so kind, Miss Mikaela, I would very much like to host a similar event when your next book is published."

I thanked him as well and assured him that Mr. Warren would be in contact with him in that regard.

"Would you perhaps join me for late afternoon refreshment?" Sir James inquired. "And your ward as well, of course."

I caught the flare of some other emotion in Lily's gaze. However, whatever she might have said— not that she wasn't outspoken —instead, she let out an excited sound and headed for the entrance to the shop.

Brodie had returned. He smiled at Lily as she took hold of his arm and steered him in our direction. His dark gaze met mine.

I did appreciate that he had returned, even several hours late. I introduced him to Sir James.

"Mr. Brodie?" he commented. "The girl mentioned your name."

"They investigate crimes together," Lily provided.

"Crimes? Most interesting," Sir James replied. "What sort of crimes?"

"Mostly murder," Lily replied before either of us could respond. "Her real name is Mrs. Brodie," she added with a smile that was anything but innocent.

I really did need to have a conversation with her about polite manners.

"Formerly with the Metropolitan Police," Brodie intervened.

Sir James didn't extend his hand, but inclined his head in acknowledgement, then turned to me.

"You seem to have made several changes in the time since we traveled together," he commented with a different expression.

I wasn't certain whether it was merely surprise or something more as Sir James nodded in Brodie's direction.

"Mikaela and I shared two travel excursions in the past that I'm certain she must have told you about," Sir James said. "Egypt, then Vienna and Switzerland. She made it far more interesting than those I usually travel with.

"And how is Lady Montgomery?" he then added. "An extraordinary woman my family has known for many years."

Still extraordinary, I thought.

"Ye have just returned, Sir James?" Brodie inquired.

"It was time. I've been away too long. One begins to miss the damp and cold. You must agree, Mr. Brodie. I detect a faint accent. Scotland perhaps?"

There was that circumspect expression again. "Not for many years," Brodie replied. "However, there are places one may go as ye have no doubt experienced in yer travels. The Greek islands for example."

"Have you been there?" Sir James replied.

"I found it to be a welcome change from the cold and damp, as ye said. I was conducting... business there."

"Most satisfactorily, one would hope."

That dark gaze met mine. "Aye."

Polite conversation, with obvious undertones. How very interesting, I thought.

For his part, Brodie was courteous and not the least intimidated by someone of Sir James' station or experiences.

However, I couldn't help but notice that reserve that he kept for those he didn't know, while Sir James was gracious and polite.

As for Lily...

"Her ladyship will be expecting us," she abruptly announced.

"Of course," Sir James commented. "Forgive me for keeping you overlong. You must remember me to her. I will be certain to call on her."

He took my hand once more then with a slight bow of his head. "It has been a pleasure to see you again, Mikaela." His smile this time seemed almost intimate, then it was gone as he turned to Brodie.

"And to meet you as well, Mr. Brodie. Good day."

Lily pulled a face as he left the shop. So much for my aunt's best efforts.

"The weather has set in," Brodie commented after Sir James had disappeared across the street. He helped us both with our coats.

I thanked the shopkeeper once more for hosting the book signing as Brodie stepped out on the sidewalk to wave down a driver.

"Yer friend seems a commendable sort," he commented as we settled ourselves in the coach and Brodie gave him the address at Sussex Square.

Commendable? I wasn't at all certain what that was supposed to mean.

"He's a friend from my first travel experience. He's quite well educated and had traveled to Egypt several times," I explained at the same time I wondered the reason I needed to explain at all.

"He's most learned in Egyptology and it made the time there far more interesting and exciting, as well as his knowledge of the places that he recommended I should see that weren't on the travel guide's itinerary."

"Ah, a young woman on her own such as on the Isle of Crete on one of yer other adventures?" Brodie suggested.

Now, what was that all about? Was I perhaps seeing a bit of male jealousy?

That was not like Brodie at all.

"He didn't purchase one of yer books," Lily said with a frown.

"It may not be the sort of book he would prefer," I replied.

"Then wot reason was he there?"

"A friend stopping by to say hello," I explained.

"Friend," she commented. "That's wot Madame said of the men who called on the ladies at the Church."

"The Church" in Edinburgh being where I first met Lily, had been converted into a brothel.

Conversations with Lily could be most enlightening. It was a glimpse of what my aunt had encountered, taking on the raising of two young girls all those years before.

"And how was your day?" I asked Brodie, diverting the conversation away from past friends, brothels, and Lily's far too observant observations.

We were much closer to Mayfair where I kept my townhouse rather than return to Sussex Square which was some distance farther.

My housekeeper Mrs. Ryan met us at the entrance, along with the aroma of supper.

Brodie shook the rain from his long hat and long coat but didn't follow us inside.

"You're not staying?" I asked.

I had hoped that we might share the evening, perhaps discuss progress in a recent inquiry I had been asked to make on behalf of an acquaintance of my aunt, and then...?

It was one of those situations that still hadn't been resolved after our return from Scotland. I continued to maintain the townhouse and we still shared the office on the Strand. There was the recent addition of Lily to the family. She frequently stayed at Sussex Square. And the cases that he took on for the Agency often required him to be away for a day or more, depending on the nature of the case.

"I need to get back to the Agency," Brodie explained.

Long days had now extended into the evenings as well. I could only guess that it was a matter of grave importance. The Special Services Agency had been formed to deal with matters beyond the usual authority of the MP and more often international affairs.

"You might stay for supper," I suggested.

"I believe that must be Mrs. Ryan's Irish stew," he shook his head with regret. "But no, I must return."

"Something very important," I suggested. I didn't bother to disguise my disappointment.

There was no one I enjoyed discussing cases or the day's work with quite so much as Brodie. He had his own thoughts on matters from years of experience with the Met and wasn't hesitant to share, unlike other men of my acquaintance who believed a woman's thoughts were best left to family and household matters.

It was one of those things that we had shared from the beginning. And then there was that *other* part of our relationship.

"I thought perhaps..."

Never shy about expressing my own thoughts, I was suddenly distracted as he slipped an arm around my waist and pulled me close.

"I would like nothing more than to stay here with ye, lass," he said, his breath gently stirring against my cheek. "But I must return. Sir Avery will be there as well, and others."

I closed my eyes and inhaled that wonderful scent about him that was always there.

"And afterward?" I asked.

His beard brushed my cheek. "It will be verra late."

"Of course," I replied.

"Ye'll be careful with the inquiries on behalf of the new

client," he added then. "If her husband has been keeping other company, he would not want it known."

"Careful as mice." When he frowned at me, I added, "I'll take Rupert with me."

I felt the faint rumble of laughter in his chest. "The smell of the damn beast would drive away anyone who might follow ye."

"He can be intimidating," I admitted.

He shook his head. "He likes ye like no other." Then looked at me with that dark gaze, his hand pressed against my cheek.

"Something we share," he added.

Considering the comparison, I wasn't at all certain that was a compliment.

He kissed me then. It was most definitely far different than a lick on the hand from the hound, and not at all the sort of thing that might be seen on the steps of one's residence in Mayfair. Or, quite possibly anywhere else.

"Go inside," he said then. "Before ye catch yer death from the cold."

And when I didn't immediately do as he asked, "What am I supposed to do with ye, when ye won't obey me?"

How amusing. He knew better.

"Ach! Ye are a stubborn one."

"And you as well, Mr. Brodie," I replied as I reached up and ran my fingers through the dark softness of his beard, then kissed him back, not at all the sort of thing a respectable lady in Mayfair would do. And I didn't give a fig if anyone saw us.

"Wot will Miss Lily have to say about yer wanton ways?" he whispered against my lips.

"Considering her previous place of residence and the

profession practiced there, I have a feeling that I might learn a thing or two from her."

There was no dissuading him from returning to the Agency. That too was something I must admit that I very much admired about him— his dedication when something important needed his attention, in spite of the fact that I would much rather he stayed.

"I look forward to that," Brodie replied.

"You would do well to remember that when you have only Alex and Sir Avery for company."

He kissed me again then returned to the coach and gave the driver instructions.

I smiled, the taste of him still on my lips as the coach disappeared through the misty rain.

How was it that I missed him already?

I entered the townhouse, hung up my coat, and informed Mrs. Ryan that Brodie would not be joining us for supper.

# Three

~~~

BRODIE WAS VERY LATE INDEED... he had not returned to the townhouse the night before. Not that it was unusual when he was working on some matter for Sir Avery and the Agency, I thought with a frown.

Although usually he was forthcoming about the matter. However, not this time. He had remained quite secretive about everything, which was not like him at all.

Mrs. Ryan provided breakfast for both Lily and myself. Then we were each off. Lily to Sussex Square for lessons much to her displeasure by the expression on her face and no few complaints. While I needed to go to the office on the Strand.

However, I reminded her that if she applied herself to her lessons, I would arrange a trip to the theater to meet my good friend Theodora Templeton. As I knew only too well, from past experience, never let it be said that a young girl couldn't be bribed when it came to her lessons.

I needed to contact Mrs. Bennett in the matter of her husband to provide her with the little information that I had— which was really no information out of the ordinary —then determine the best course to pursue. If we even had a case in the matter.

It was very possible that all of this was merely exaggeration on the part of Mrs. Bennett— a husband dedicated to his work and nothing more.

Brodie and I had experience in these matters. The best we could do was provide information then let the client decide the course of action to be taken. Very often it was no action at all on the part of the woman in the relationship.

That was most unfortunate. However there was that whole expectation of society when it came to extramarital affairs, soldiering on as they say to avoid a scandal.

The reality was that few women, other than those of my aunt's or my sister's acquaintance, had the means to support themselves after a divorce.

Then, there was the scandal of divorce which my sister had endured for a short while. After just so much gossip she had adopted my habit of telling the offensive person to sod off and then simply walked away.

With my independence, my travels, and the novels I wrote, it was a time-tested solution that actually worked quite well.

I had to admit there was something quite satisfying about the expression on the offending person's face as they stammered and tut-tutted that they had never been so offended.

It was one of the few reasons that I had hesitated when Brodie first proposed. I didn't need a man to define who I was. I didn't need a man to support me. I most certainly didn't need a man who was determined to keep me in my place.

God knows that Brodie could be stubborn and quite old fashioned about some things. He was also the most challenging man I had ever met. However, he made me think, not merely to humor me.

He valued my thoughts and my opinions, often seeking them out or adding his own observations to the lists that I made. He accepted me the way I was, though not without reminders from time to time regarding how obstinate I could be.

In short, he didn't attempt to change me, although he did disapprove of some of the things I did from time to time.

No, I most certainly didn't need a man.

The problem was quite simply that I wanted the man. More than any man I had ever met or known. In spite of his grumbling and grousing from time to time, even outright disapproval which I usually chose to ignore.

I wanted him to challenge me with his own thoughts and ideas. I didn't mind when he became angry with me, because I actually understood where it came from. And perhaps the most important part, aside from the fact that he made my toes curl, was that he valued me in a way that no man ever had.

So, what was an enlightened, independent woman to do?

However, at present, I would have valued him a great deal more had he returned to Mayfair the night before. Since he had not and there was business to attend to— the business of our latest inquiry case —I arrived at the Strand with sufficient food sent along in a basket by Mrs. Ryan for Mr. Cavendish and Rupert the hound.

It had become a habit that Mr. Cavendish thoroughly appreciated. As for the hound? One could only judge by his enthusiasm as he nosed about for one of her biscuits with a tin of stew from supper the night before for Mr. Cavendish.

Her recipe, handed down from her Irish mother, included chunks of beef rather than mutton which I was not fond of. However I did so appreciate her skill in that regard since I did not cook beyond a scramble of eggs or burnt muffin.

"Mr. Brodie was by late last night for a time," Mr. Cavendish informed as I sent the driver on his way.

"Musta been near two or three of the mornin'," he added. "Met with Mr. Conner. Seemed a bit unusual that time o' the night."

Unusual indeed, I thought.

"Did he perhaps leave a message?" I asked.

"Said something about an inquiry case you were makin', and if you was to go off on yer own I was to see that you took the hound with you. He musta thought it could be dangerous for you."

I had taken myself off on my own in our previous inquiries, quite safe for the most part.

"He did say that he left the revolver in the desk for you as well," Mr. Cavendish added.

The hound and now I was to take a revolver. It wasn't like Brodie to be overprotective, like some mother hen as the saying went.

However, there was no point in arguing the matter with Mr. Cavendish. He was merely passing the message along.

I glanced down at Rupert. He was presently dozing at the entrance to the alcove where he usually spent the night.

"He was out late as well," Mr. Cavendish informed me. "Came back this morning, rougher than a badger's arse, and been there ever since."

That was a most colorful description. I wondered how Mr. Cavendish might know that particular aspect regarding a badger. There was not so much as an eye cracked open by the hound.

Late, indeed. In consideration of the things he had been known to drag back to the alcove in the past, one could only imagine where he'd been.

"He'll be right as the rain though when you're ready to leave, miss."

I had my doubts as the hound was presently snoring loud enough even over the usual noise from the street this time of the morning.

Right as rain, indeed.

"Look for a message on the landing," Mr. Cavendish added. "It was brought round first thing by one of them courier services."

He gestured overhead to the second-floor landing.

Climbing the stairs to deliver the message was not an option due to an injury some years before that had taken both of his legs at the knees. Therefore messages that were delivered were either announced by the rope pull attached to a bell on the landing if Brodie or myself were about. If not, it was sent aloft, tucked in an empty whisky bottle from my aunt's estate at Old Lodge in the north of Scotland.

The message was rolled and inserted into the bottle. A cord was then tied about the neck of the bottle and it was sent aloft to the second-floor landing at the end of a rope by way of a pulley. It really was quite ingenious.

"How are you getting along with the new platform Brodie had made for you?" I inquired before turning to the stairs.

The previous one that he wheeled about the streets of London on had been a crude affair that at least gave Mr. Cavendish mobility.

It had been destroyed in a previous case and Brodie had replaced it with a fine one made of hickory with wheels affixed with rubber and a thick carpet on the platform.

However, the carpet was easily soaked by the weather and Mr. Cavendish had reluctantly discarded it. He had commandeered a lady's padded undergarment from one of the seconds shops in the East End.

Miss Effie, a friend at the Public House across the way had stitched the pads into the bottom of his trousers providing a comfortable change for him.

"The cushion is right fine, helps ease the misery in me bones," he replied. "Thanks to Miss Effie," he added. "She's a good woman."

A good woman indeed. Did I sense a hint of something more behind that comment?

Prior to my association with Brodie, Mr. Cavendish was known to take up lodging in the storeroom behind the Public House when the weather turned bad.

Miss Effie was a widow, having lost her husband some time earlier. Brodie had paid the rent on her flat in the past before she found work at the Public House. I was aware he still supplemented her wages from time to time.

She had returned the favor in a roundabout way, by arranging for the back door to the storeroom at the Public House to be left unlocked for Mr. Cavendish when storms rolled in from the river and flooded the streets and sidewalks.

There was a sound from the hound now as I reached the stairs. However, he had merely rolled over onto his back and continued his snoring, much like someone sleeping it off.

So much for accompanying me on my travels about London.

"The biscuits you brought will ease his temper when he wakens," Mr. Cavendish commented.

I had my doubts as I climbed the stairs to the second-floor landing and retrieved the message that Mr. Cavendish had tucked into the neck of the bottle. It was from Helen Bennett.

*Miss Forsythe, please contact me as soon as you receive this. I need to meet with you. The situation has become most serious.*
*Helen Bennett*

That did sound quite ominous, I thought.

I had met with her previously in the matter of her husband's absences over the past several weeks.

At first those absences had not seemed unusual as he frequently worked long hours that extended into the evening. But those absences had become more frequent over the past few weeks and with only the same explanation each time that it was his *"work."*

Joseph Bennett was a physician and surgeon. It seemed plausible that his work made demands on his time.

I had made the usual inquiries at his office and at the club he was known to frequent. It appeared that he left the office at the usual hour most days, however he had not attended his club in some time.

Although that did not answer the question as to where he went when he was not at his office, the hospital, or his club, I had not found anything amiss.

His office assistant, an older woman by the name of Mary Bishop who attended patients as well as staff I spoke with at St. Thomas' Hospital, had not noticed anything different in his habits. Long hours, the administrator of the hospital explained, were not unusual.

As for Helen Bennett, she did not appear to be someone given to hysterics over a missed supper or two. She was intelligent, quite calm in her manner, and used to the callings of her husband's profession that occasionally required him to be at some function or called away with the lectures he gave.

When we met previously there had been a noticeable

concern over her husband's increased absences, but this was now more than mere concern and the growing suspicion that he might be *keeping company* elsewhere as she put it at the time.

I had found no indication of that, having become quite familiar with the usual signs of a philandering husband in the matter of my sister's case, and the early experience with our own father.

By all accounts, Dr. Bennett was a dedicated physician, lecturer, and prominent member of the Medical Society of London.

He had done extensive research in the treatment and after-care of wounds suffered by those in the military in campaigns in Burma and more recently in the Sudan, and frequently lectured on advances in such things.

Our previous acquaintance with a captain of the Royal Fusiliers, who had been injured in one of those confrontations and returned to London, had been the benefactor of some of those advances.

Instead of losing his injured leg as would have happened in the past, he had gone through restorative surgery and was assured of the returned use of the limb.

I had also made inquiries about the Bennett family, in case there might be any difficulties there— obligations to a family member that might have made a demand on Dr. Bennett's time.

His parents were long deceased and there was only a sister who had moved with her husband to the United States. The distance precluded any concern in that regard. And Mrs. Bennett had not indicated any difficulty there.

Mrs. Bennett was from a notable family. Her father had been an architect and had designed the first residences constructed in Belgrave Square where she and her husband now lived.

While the square and the surrounding area was known for those of the upper class who lived there, I did not have the impression that Dr. and Mrs. Bennett lived lavishly or beyond their means. There did not seem to be any sort of financial difficulty. A housekeeper answered my telephone call to the Bennett residence and it was immediately picked up by Mrs. Bennett.

I could hear the tension in her voice. She was quite upset however, but did not want to discuss whatever it was that had happened over the telephone, or obviously in the presence of servants.

I agreed to meet with her promptly.

I added a brief note to the chalkboard— a habit that had driven Brodie quite crazy when we first worked together. He kept details in his head, as he had explained at the time, far more efficient when going about London on some matter or the other.

However, he was forced to admit that my notes were quite efficient when the two of us were working on an inquiry case. It was his way of acknowledging that I had contributed important aspects to that particular case. Stubborn man.

I tucked Mrs. Bennett's note into my bag and was almost out the door of the office when I remembered Mr. Cavendish's message from Brodie.

Oh, bother, I thought as I returned to the desk and retrieved the revolver, what Brodie called a "pocket pistol."

It was small enough to tuck into my bag and somewhat lighter than the one he usually carried. A gift he told me at the time, since I had a habit of getting myself into certain situations. He was a bit put off by my martial art skills, acquired on a previous visit to the Far East.

*"There's no need for ye to engage with a criminal. Use the pistol if ye need to."*

He had proceeded to provide a lesson in the proper loading and handling of the weapon at my aunt's estate at Sussex Square, a private location where the Metropolitan Police were not likely to be called upon to investigate.

To say that I was a most excellent student is an understatement. I had taken two practice shots in order to compensate for the weight and the accuracy of the weapon, then proceeded to put an additional four rounds in the center of the target.

There had been the requisite muttering with a handful of curses thrown in for good measure on Brodie's part afterward.

*"I suppose ye learned that from her ladyship,"* he snapped when the lesson was over.

*"She is quite accomplished, although she much prefers the saber. In her youth she bested several men in competition, dressed in disguise so that she would not be disqualified."*

There had been more muttering at that, along with, *"No surprise why the woman is still unmarried. She undoubtedly killed off any serious suitor.*

*"I have to admit,"* he then added. *"I was not aware that such things were family traits. Although I am grateful that ye have the skill, considerin' yer inclination for finding trouble."*

I had reminded him that the "trouble" he was referring to was a matter I was forced to take care of considering his preoccupation elsewhere at the time.

It was a matter that was still up for discussion from time to time.

While I was fairly certain that calling on Mrs. Bennett did not present a danger of any kind, I went ahead and tucked the pistol into my bag. No point in poking the bear— Brodie being the bear as it were.

The hound was a different matter. Brodie had also insisted that I take the hound with me whenever I was out and about in London on an inquiry case.

One look at Rupert as I left the office and descended the steps to the street, and I was doubtful that he would be well received at Belgrave Square. He did lack a certain appropriate presentation, not to mention that most people did not go about London with a guard hound.

The closest thing might be the Pekingese dogs that some women tucked under their arms, a bit of fluff that hardly resembled a dog at all with bows and baubles tied about their necks.

As a child I had been very familiar with my father's hunting dogs that Rupert most closely resembled, including the mud. In the hound's case the somewhat overripe smell was undoubtedly from the day's catch at the docks.

"Aye," Mr. Cavendish acknowledged, as he waived down a cab for me. "Mr. Brodie did mention that ye were to take the beast with ye."

I looked at "the beast," quite alert now from his morning nap no doubt at the prospect of an adventure.

While I had my doubts, I was forced to admit that he had acquitted himself quite admirably in the past during a particularly nasty investigation. In short, he had undoubtedly saved my life, or at least prevented substantial injury.

It was, of course, difficult to imagine at present as he sat at my feet, tongue hanging out the side of his mouth, with what appeared to be a grin once one got past the appearance of all those teeth.

"Oh, very well," I conceded as the driver arrived. I held

open the gate and the hound promptly jumped inside which brought a frown from atop the cab.

I gave the driver the address at Belgrave Square, then climbed in as well.

Mr. Cavendish nodded. "He's just protectin' his own," he commented as he turned and paddled back from the sidewalk on his rolling platform.

Protecting his own?

Unless the hound had developed some sort of human emotional sense. I doubted that. Although I could have sworn otherwise with that grin, most particularly when he had caught something particularly foul. However, I had the distinct feeling that Mr. Cavendish was not referring to the hound.

We arrived at Number 32 Belgrave Square in good time. I paid the driver, then looked down at the hound. It seemed unlikely that he would be welcome in the Bennett residence. Or at the square for that matter, as a gentleman in a long coat and hat glanced our way with a critical expression as he passed by.

"Are you quite all right, miss?" he asked with a wary eye toward Rupert.

The hound did bring out that sort of comment from people beyond the Strand. However, those who frequented the area were quite accustomed to seeing him about.

"Yes, of course," I replied and thanked him, which brought the usual sort of response as the gentleman turned and went about his way, with a cautious glance back over his shoulder.

"Filthy beast!"

I could have sworn the hound was most pleased with himself.

"Stay," I told him, a statement that would have worked with my father's well-trained hunting hounds. However...

"Stay, or there will be no more biscuits," I added.

Quite amazingly, the hound sat down and stared back at me with what I could only guess was an expectant expression, then proceeded to lay down, head resting on outstretched paws alongside the wrought iron fence at the entrance to the building.

"Good boy," I told him.

I could only imagine what my friend Templeton's response would have been to my conversation with the hound, since she was quite familiar with conversing with Ziggy, her four-and-a-half-foot long iguana that had been given to her after one of her tours.

Ziggy was currently residing in the London Zoo after escaping and causing some excitement about the city. The last I had spoken with Templeton, she was quite concerned for him.

*"They don't understand how sensitive he is. He appears quite lonely,"* she had commented after a recent visit.

The Bennett housekeeper answered the bell pull. With a look back at the hound, still stretched out along the fence, I entered the residence for my meeting with Helen Bennett.

As I said, she did not give the impression of one with nothing better to do than worry endlessly about everything. Even now, after that note and hearing the sound of her voice over the telephone, she appeared quite calm as she thanked me for meeting with her on such short notice.

Her housekeeper served tea, then was politely excused, the doors to the parlor closed.

Helen Bennett set her cup down. The only outward sign of emotion was in the faint trembling of her hands as she tightly folded them.

"Dr. Bennett has not returned at all since last we spoke," she informed me in a lowered voice.

That was two days earlier. Prior to that, he returned often late of the night with no explanation to his wife. And now, he had not returned at all.

"Has there been any communication from him?" I asked. "Anything that he might have mentioned the last time, perhaps regarding some matter that would keep him away for a length of time?"

She shook her head. "I sent round a message to his office at the hospital and was informed that they had not heard from him. His assistant assured me that they would let me know if they had word from him."

I then asked questions I had previously asked, having discovered in the past that one might often forget some small detail in the midst of a trying situation. It was often something that might seem unimportant at the time, but might offer a clue about a person's thoughts or actions.

While I was somewhat a student of people's manners and expressions, it was Brodie who had taught me the importance of a somewhat nervous gesture or a distracted gaze from his work with the Met and years spent on the streets of London. Quite invaluable in our inquiry cases.

It was a sad fact that people often lied or completely denied knowing anything about a situation, often to protect themselves. But those small movements, even something as insignificant as a twitch, or a glance away often betrayed the lie.

"What about something he might have said, perhaps an offhand remark, or possibly a change in his manner? Anything that might have seemed different.

"Was he perhaps impatient with the servants? Or short-tempered over something?"

She appeared to think back over that last night when he had returned.

"There was something... however, I had seen it before and thought nothing of it at the time."

"Anything at all might be useful," I replied.

"I don't usually question him about his work at the hospital, however with everything the past two months... And then he left again that same evening and didn't return."

There was a trembling in her voice as she seemed to gather herself.

"I asked him if it was some matter at the hospital," she replied. "That seemed the most likely situation..."

Other than the possibility that he was meeting someone— a woman perhaps?

"He became very angry, and that is not like him at all. Joseph is a very reserved, quiet man. I've never known him to become angry with anyone..."

But he had that last night.

"He said that it was not my place to question him. He has never said anything like that to me before. He was most agitated."

"Did he offer any explanation?"

"He said it was nothing for me to be concerned about. Then, he left and didn't return."

She described him as a reserved, quiet man, who became angry at a simple question, his manner quite unusual. Then commented that it was nothing for her to be concerned about.

The question was— why the uncharacteristic outburst? Because he didn't want her asking more questions that he either didn't care to or wasn't prepared to answer? If so, for what reason?

Was it an affair as Helen Bennett had initially suspected? Or was it something else? Something that he didn't want her to know anything about?

"What about any communication he might have made that last evening from here?" I then asked. "Perhaps a telephone conversation? Or some message he received that might have upset him?"

Once again, Helen Bennett shook her head.

"There was nothing."

Her voice trailed off in a whisper that conveyed so much— uncertainty, doubt, desperation. I felt all of those emotions for her. I could only imagine if the circumstances were my own and Brodie's.

I reached out and covered her hand with mine.

"We will do everything we can to learn what has happened."

"How?" she asked, looking up at me with tear-filled eyes.

"There are ways..." I thought of Brodie's skill in such matters, as well as those who had assisted us in the past. It was as much as I could give her for now.

I had learned little more in my meeting with Helen Bennett, but that little amount might provide a valuable clue as to the good doctor's movements that last day.

It required a return visit to the hospital where he was part of the staff. But first I needed to make a visit to Mr. Brimley, the chemist in the East End who had been helpful with matters in the past.

He had studied at King's College and initially pursued the profession of physician. Although circumstances had changed his path so to speak, he still had a very close association with his fellow students who were now among the most prominent physicians in London.

Mr. Brimley had a shop in the poorest part of London where he administered to the needs of the people there—

dispensing powders and pills, seeing to the needs of women and children, and occasionally stitching a wound.

I could attest to his expert skills in that regard. There were only two small scars from the bullet when I was shot in the course of my first investigation with Brodie.

The hound sat up as I left the Bennett residence, quite surprising me that he was still there given his wandering ways and with new streets to scavenge.

"Good boy," I told him. He fell into step beside me as I went to the corner of the square to find a cab.

Mr. Brimley always had a good specimen for the hound.

# *Four*

## THE AGENCY, TOWER OF LONDON

ANGUS BRODIE ROLLED his head against the stiffness in the back of his neck from too many hours going back through everything that was known, and a great deal more that wasn't known.

It was very near midday, and he had been at it for verra near twenty-four hours with the latest information Sir Avery had received from Luxembourg.

The information was regarding a man named Soropkin who was supposedly responsible for several incidents on the continent, the sort of individual who lived in the shadows, until he was ready to strike.

Soropkin was Lithuanian by birth but called no place home. He was the sort of person with no loyalty to any place or anyone. He moved in the shadows in whatever city he happened to be in, constantly moving about, never in one place longer than it took to plan the next attack against those in power. Sir Avery's people on the continent had been working with their sources regarding an obscure bit of information they had received months earlier in that shadowy world most people didn't know existed. Where a life was worth less than the mud on the bottom of a man's boot, and anything and anyone could be purchased or disposed of.

"Do ye trust the information?" Brodie had asked Sir Avery at the time.

"I trust our sources and the amount of money they receive for the information they provide."

"What about others who might pay more for that information?" Brodie had asked, having experience in such matters.

"That is where you come in. You know people on the street. You need to find those at the lowest levels who would have knowledge of this."

That was over two months ago, before he left for Edinburgh. It was an obscure piece of information that might have meant something. Or nothing.

He had passed what he had learned on to Sir Avery before he left London, unaware of its importance at the time and with little concern over it— a rumor among dozens of others heard on the street. There were other matters that pulled him back to Edinburgh, that had been waiting for verra near thirty years.

That was then, this was now.

There was a new urgency as the latest information the Agency had received from Luxembourg and decoded was verra near two weeks old with a warning about something that had been described as dangerous with far-reaching consequences.

Only another rumor like so many others the Agency followed up on?

However, Sir Avery wanted him to check with his sources on the street. More than that he wouldn't say. It was an aspect of the work the Agency did that he found to be off-putting.

Sir Avery provided just enough information to send him

off in a particular direction with little more to go on— that *"little more"* could be dangerous.

It was like being in a street fight with one hand tied behind his back, and something he didn't care for. It was Mr. Sinclair who had provided more information in a hastily whispered comment.

It seemed the "event" that was rumored was a possible assassination attempt that Soropkin was involved in. But against who?

It wasn't the first time. A previous inquiry case had exposed a threat against the Prince of Wales. And then, there had been the attempts in the past against the Queen.

That information, Brodie had been able to learn from bits and pieces of information in the past, came from a network of those the Agency— and therefore the Crown, paid to keep them informed about increasing unrest in Europe.

It came by way of coded messages in telegrams as well as bits of information in obscure telephone calls that Alex revealed the Agency was able to listen to through new equipment that had been invented. And then there were messages intercepted, like this last one, often at great cost.

"What about the man, who originally provided the information some time ago?" he had then asked Alex.

"Nothing has been heard from him since that first message, even with the amount of money he was promised. He's a greedy sort and has always had something to send us. But there's been nothing more."

Sir Avery hadn't shared that with him, something that might mean nothing at all.

On the other hand, it might mean that there was someone who was willing to pay more, that the information first received was just a rumor, or that the man's communication with London had been exposed, and he was dead.

He had thanked Alex for the additional information then set out to learn what he could about Soropkin, in anything that might be overheard on the streets— long hours that often went far into the night. He had said nothing about it to Mikaela.

He worked those sorts of hours and more with the Met, and in private inquiries on behalf of clients. He was accustomed to it. One did the work until the work was done. And this new urgency was like searching for needles in haystacks as someone would have reminded him.

That particular someone would have been the first person to understand, to give her thoughts on the matter and then plunge into the middle of it.

Mikaela— intelligent, stubborn, fearless... with a habit for ending up in the middle of things, dangerous things that made him want to shake some sense into her, then hold onto her to make certain she was safe.

She was safe now, or as safe as she could possibly be all things considered, off on her own inquiry case.

He could well imagine her with her notebook and pen. That direct way she had of obtaining information. The case— a husband, a physician, who had been keeping late hours and being most secretive, the wife certain there must be another woman involved.

Then again, he thought, knowing Mikaela's past experience with her own father, it might be dangerous for the poor man when she finally learned his whereabouts and the reason for it.

"Contact the priest again," Sir Avery was telling him now.

The priest was one of his sources.

"Call me if he's heard anything more, then go home and get some sleep."

He had placed a call to Father Sebastian and asked to meet with him before he left the Tower.

Now, as he made his way from that ancient fortress he thought of Sir Avery's parting comment— "go home and get some sleep."

Home. At present that might be the office on the Strand or Mikaela's townhouse in Mayfair.

It didn't matter. He'd spent his life on the streets and slept in places that were best forgotten before joining the London Police. Afterward there had been a small flat, then the office on the Strand best suited his needs.

It didn't matter, he thought again, as long as she was there, with her notes, and questions, and suggestions. Even when she put herself into situations where she had no business. She would have argued that with him.

He found a driver and gave him the location in Whitechapel.

The German Catholic Mission Church had served the immigrant community that had grown over the past several years, ministering to the poor, providing a haven of faith for those who had little else.

Brodie had met Father Sebastian in the course of a previous investigation some years before, when the priest was asked to provide last rites over a young girl who had been brutally used and then left to die on the streets.

The priest had arrived in the East End over twenty years earlier, with little more than a Bible and his faith. In that time he had established a school for orphan children and helped families as best he could.

*"God does not ask whether Catholic, Methodist, or Jew,"* Father Sebastian once told him. *"He accepts all, and I can do no less."*

After that first, Brodie had made contributions to the church in his mother's name. She had been baptized in the faith and believed in a merciful and protective God, even with her dying breath.

His own beliefs were more circumspect, influenced by the streets as a boy after her death and then in London. With what he saw on the streets, he thought that God might very well not exist at all.

*"It is not the big miracles,"* Father Sebastian had reminded him in one of their conversations. *"But the small everyday miracles— a life saved, a wrong that is set right, food and clothes for those who have none."*

Brodie didn't believe that the clothes he delivered from a woman who ran the seconds shop in Holborn from time to time for children at the school were a miracle. It was simply something that he could do.

Then there was what had waited in Edinburgh, finding his mother's murderer, and the fire for revenge that had burned in him since he was a lad.

Father Sebastian had cautioned him about taking revenge on that last visit before Brodie left. It was not wrong to seek justice he explained, but revenge for the sake of revenge was a sin.

In the end he didn't know whether it was justice or revenge he'd found in Edinburgh. Afterward, he had spoken of it with Mikaela at Old Lodge in the north of Scotland before returning to London.

*"And your choice would have been to simply let the man go about destroying other lives to protect himself and his career after murdering your mother when she refused him? And the others who knew what happened that night?*

*"What about Kip?"* she had then asked of the boy from a

previous inquiry case who had verra nearly died, and yet they had found the persons responsible and he supposed there was some justice in that, the possibility that other children— at least a few of them, wouldn't suffer or be used as the lad had been.

*"And what about Templeton?"* she asked of her friend. *"Would you have simply let her be tried for a murder she did not commit?"*

*"Well there was the damned lizard,"* he had admitted. *"Dangerous beast. It would have served her right."*

*"Ziggy is an iguana,"* she had corrected him. *"And he was not at all dangerous. He's an herbivore— he eats only plants."*

He wasn't certain he believed that given his encounters with the creature. But he believed in the woman who had dropped into his life like a storm and took away his doubts about his reasons for going to Edinburgh.

Father Sebastian had sent word a week ago when it seemed that everything had gone quiet.

*"It was told to me in confession,"* the priest had said when he met with him afterward.

*"I have prayed over it. As you well know, my friend, that which is told in confession is inviolate and I am bound to keep secret. However, this seemed most serious and I cannot condone the taking of innocent lives."*

It was then Father Sebastian told him what it was that he had heard in confession— a conversation overheard by a man on the voyage to London that troubled him deeply, and the choice the priest was forced to make to break his vow of silence regarding confession.

The man who had come to him, a tailor by the name of Anatole, was traveling from Budapest with his wife and young son.

With anarchist groups terrorizing the city, it had become too dangerous for them to remain in the country where they were born.

His wife's brother had immigrated to London the year before and encouraged them in letters to leave.

Once the decision was made, they traveled from Budapest to Paris, then to LeHavre where they found passage to London.

It was on that trip from LeHavre that Anatole overheard a conversation between two men.

The tailor had stumbled upon them on a walk about the deck one night and had then hidden himself because of the words he'd overheard.

The two men spoke of an event that had been set in motion, with information one man was to take to others once they arrived in London. Then a packet with something inside was exchanged.

Payment for seeing that the information was delivered, perhaps?

The tailor did not know, but the men's manner, a phrase he picked up on even in his broken English— *"They will pay in blood"* —had convinced him that it was something dangerous.

In addition, there was a note, to be delivered once the one man arrived in London.

Was there anything else the tailor mentioned? Anything that might tell them what the event was?

The priest nodded. *"That it would not be suspected with the coming holiday celebrations. But he saw something in addition to that message. It was a tattoo on the wrist of one of the men— that looked like a black hand."*

There had also been a name, *Soropkin.*

*"I know this name as well,"* Father Sebastian had continued, *"from the old country. The man is an assassin. If what the tailor*

*overheard is true, I fear something will happen here and very soon."*

From what Brodie had learned at the Agency, Soropkin had once been the leader of an anarchist group responsible for assassinations in France and Spain. And the tattoo the tailor had seen was the mark of the anarchist movement found on posters in several cities.

There had been warnings circulated by the Metropolitan Police several years earlier to be vigilant regarding individuals who might have arrived in London in the aftermath of those assassinations.

The first inquiry case with Mikaela in the disappearance of her sister, had exposed individuals with anarchist ties.

Brodie had thanked the priest and promised to keep the fact that the information came through confession a secret when he had first asked Alex Sinclair if there had been any recent information about a new threat or plot.

*"Nothing,"* Alex had replied at the time. *"It's been very quiet."*

Perhaps too quiet, Brodie thought and put out word to his friend, Munro, who often came in contact with merchants and workmen at the warehouses along the riverfront as manager of Lady Montgomery's estates.

He'd also put out word with Mr. Conner who he'd worked with before he retired. Mr. Conner knew people at the docks from his time with the MET and often lifted a pint with them. Both were men he could trust to keep the information to themselves.

*"Anything that might indicate any activity someone doesna want the authorities to know about, unusual shipments that aren't on a manifest, names that might have surfaced again that might be familiar from previous cases."*

"*Is there a particular person we're lookin' for?*" Munro asked.

He gave them the name the tailor had overheard—Soropkin.

Conner had cursed. "*I'm not fond of the upper classes and the hold they keep on the working man, as you well know,*" he commented.

"*However, I had hoped that Soropkin was no longer among the living.*" Conner shook his head then continued.

"*Too many good men have ended up dead because of him. And to my way of thinkin' the change that he wants to bring about will cost too many lives of innocent people,*" he spat out.

"*It makes one wonder if that one was any better than those of the upper classes? In it for himself and only wears a different boot?*

"*Now you tell me that he may still be alive, and here in London?*"

Brodie understood only too well, as did Munro. They both came from the streets. They had seen the poverty and crime every day. They had lived it, and there was the long and painful history of Scotland at the mercy of English authority.

A different boot, Conner called it.

"*What about Miss Mikaela?*" Munro had asked. "*She might be able to learn something from those she knows. The man at the canal docks? He's the sort who knows a great deal about what comes into the country.*"

Captain Turner was a man who had served thirty years on merchant ships and was then forced to retire after a shipboard accident took his leg. He ran the canal boats that brought goods in from the country and took on passengers as well.

Captain Tom, as she referred to him from a past acquaintance, also operated a bit of smuggling according to what Brodie had learned about the man.

*"No!"* his answer was firm. At the look both men gave him he had added, *"She's not to be involved in this. She has another inquiry she is working at present."*

Munro nodded. *"I wish ye luck with that."*

He knew Munro was right. He was going to need more than luck when it came to keeping her out of this.

Considering what the Agency had learned along with that conversation overheard by the tailor, it was safe to assume there was something planned that might have serious repercussions. Sir Avery had also shared that there had been more recent rumors from other sources that something might be planned against the Crown.

Was it the Black Hand? There was reason to suspect that it was a possibility.

Mikaela had spoken of the organization; it was the first he heard it was mentioned. There had been a deadly confrontation in Budapest between the anarchists and authorities on one of her travels a handful of years earlier.

That information had been useful at the time.

There was more to it now, of course, he was willing to admit. For him everything had changed with that simple ceremony in Edinburgh, a piece of paper with their names, a "contract" she had commented at the time with her usual penchant for being sarcastic. But for him, it was more than that.

Then weeks after those first rumors, and a piece of information passed to him by Mr. Dooley, a man he worked with in his years with the Met. The information came by way of a report filed by the officers on the watch the night before.

They'd been called when a body was found in Holborn. A man by the name of Anatole had been stabbed to death. He had been found in the back room of a tailor's shop by the owner.

Robbery? An assault that ended badly? Common enough in parts of London. Except for the man's name, a name that was familiar from the information Father Sebastian had given him.

Coincidence? Another man named Anatole? However, a man by that name who was also a tailor?

He didn't believe in coincidences. Experience had taught him there was no such thing.

He hadn't had a chance to speak with the man from the confessional yet, and thought then of Father Sebastian.

If the attack wasn't about robbery, then what was it? Was it possible that someone else knew of the man's confession to Father Sebastian?

The church was quiet this hour of the evening in the middle of the week. Those who attended to confess their sins long since gone with only a handful of worshippers who knelt among the pews, perhaps those on their way home from work, or those who had no other place to go.

There was a stand near the altar with rows of candles that had been lit below a sculptured scene.

A *frieze*, Mikaela had explained at another church in Edinburgh during an inquiry case. They depicted various scenes from the Bible, according to what she told him. His time in such places, admittedly, had been limited.

*"I suppose people find comfort in such things,"* she had remarked at the time. *"Places filled with artwork, frescoes and priceless objects while lives are ruined, and children starve."*

That had surprised him. It came, he supposed, from her own past and her travels to those faraway places that gave her that point of view. That and her bloody independence that had a way of getting her into trouble from time to time.

Although she would have argued that *"trouble"* as he saw it, was merely doing something because she could. And that brought him back around to the small ceremony, merely signing a piece of paper in Edinburgh.

She deserved more, he thought at the time. A church ceremony, even with his somewhat questionable past, a fine gown to wear, and something more than the plain ring he had placed on her hand.

In her usual way, she had assured him that she didna need a church or a priest or vicar for something that was between two people.

And the license? A formality on paper to satisfy the local magistrate.

She didna need a piece of paper, she told him, only that he not get himself kilt any time soon.

He had laughed and asked the same of her— an odd way, he'd thought at the time, to begin this new part of their partnership.

He made his way now through the nave to the door at the back of the altar that led to the anteroom where Father Sebastian met privately with parishioners or prepared for his next service.

He entered the short hallway, then continued down the hall to the small office at the end. The door was slightly ajar. He knocked in case the priest was with someone, then pushed open the door when there was no answer.

Father Sebastian was there, sprawled on the floor.

Light from the hallway glistened upon the dark stain that

spread beneath him. One hand reached out across the slate stones on the floor.

An attempt to protect himself? Or possibly a last act of absolution for the murderer as the priest lay dying?

The attack had apparently come as Father Sebastian returned to the office from afternoon prayers or perhaps meeting with one of his parishioners.

Was it the same person who killed the tailor? Or could it have been one of those Brodie had seen in the church.

For money?

The church was poor. He doubted there was anything in the offering plate.

For food or shelter?

Father Sebastian would have shared his last crust of bread and provided a place for anyone in need.

Brodie cursed as he knelt beside the priest and felt for a pulse even though he already knew what he would find.

His eyes narrowed. With only the light from the single electric in the hallway, a bloodied image appeared almost black on the slate stone beside the priest's outstretched arm.

It was the image of a hand in the priest's own blood that appeared almost black in the meager light.

A coincidence? Nothing more than the priest's outstretched hand covered in blood as he lay dying?

Or was it a message?

The priest had entrusted him with information learned through confession out of concern for the tailor. Both were now dead.

Brodie returned to the nave. Had the people there perhaps heard or seen something? Was the murderer possibly there among them?

An elderly man looked up briefly then returned to his

prayers. An old woman sat silently, beads clutched in her hands. Another woman, obviously unwell by the pallor of her face attempted to quiet the child beside her.

From years of experience none of them looked as though they were capable of murdering the priest.

Had they perhaps seen something?

He approached the older man. He used the excuse of looking for a friend he was supposed to meet there. The man shook his head.

He had been there for the good part of an hour. There had been no one else, other than those Brodie saw.

Whoever had been there was now gone.

And it was apparent that the rumors they'd been following were rumors no more.

# Five

"TELL ME, Miss Mikaela, what brings you to my shop this late in the afternoon?" Mr. Brimley asked as I sat at the desk in his small office that was hardly more than part of the storeroom at the back of his shop while Rupert was presently in the company of Mr. Brimley's assistant, Sara.

The hound seemed to have a particular fondness for the ladies. In another life perhaps as a human? If one believed in those things, I imagined he would have been quite the rake.

"Dr. Joseph Bennett, you say?" Mr. Brimley nodded as he poured two mugs of coffee and handed one to me.

"I know of the man. He studied at King's College and is an associate professor of medicine there as well as his lectures at Oxford. He's well-known both as a physician and a surgeon," he continued.

"He has made enormous contributions with reconstructive surgery for those injured in catastrophic accidents as well as the war wounded, though I've never met the man." He made a visual sweep of the office and the shop beyond.

"This is not the sort of place a man of his skill and achievements might frequent." A circumspect smile appeared. "And you're making inquiries for the family, you say?"

I nodded. "What do you know about the sort of person he is?"

"From what I've heard he's very dedicated and well respected. However," he added with that circumspect look again, "if you are asking me about the man himself, I cannot say." He was thoughtful.

"There is someone who might be able to tell you. Dr. Pennington would know more about the man. They've shared joint lectures, I believe. Most particularly regarding the military who returned after injury in India or some other place. There was also some travel to France that I read about, and a series of lectures he gave at some university after he published a book about his works."

A book. How very interesting, I thought.

What might that tell me about the man, if anything?

I had met Dr. Pennington. He had provided valuable information in a previous case. In one of those ways that life makes odd friendships, Mr. Brimley and Dr. Pennington had met in medical school, and remained close even after Mr. Brimley was forced to withdraw before completing his courses and had opened his shop in one of the poorest areas of London.

"I will send round a message and let him know that you will be calling on him," Mr. Brimley added.

It was quite late when I left the chemist's shop with Rupert. I went to the office on the Strand, hoping that I might find Brodie. However, Mr. Cavendish informed me that he had not returned.

I went up to the office, disappointed, as I was accustomed to sharing what I had learned with him in our inquiry cases.

There was more to it, of course, when I was honest with myself and chose to examine my disappointment.

We had a somewhat unusual arrangement. Partners in the inquiry cases the past two years to be certain. But that was only part of it, most recently of course, with that little ceremony in the north of Scotland. Something I had most certainly never considered for myself.

The truth, when I was willing to admit it, was that I missed him. I missed our exchanges at the end of the day here at the office on the Strand. I missed the way there was usually a fire burning in the coal stove and possibly a bottle of Old Lodge with two glasses on his desk.

I had become accustomed to his habits, his challenges to my thoughts, even his grumbling and grousing over some matter. Not to mention the messiness atop his desk that I was constantly straightening, the way his hair curled over his collar for lack of a trim, and that way he had of looking at me over the edge of his glass.

Admittedly, there was often a frown, those dark eyes narrowed almost as if he was attempting to figure out what sort of species I was with my questions and comments. Then there were the other times when that frown and that dark gaze meant something far different.

In spite of my self-doubts, I had grown accustomed to Brodie. The office seemed empty without him when it had never seemed so before.

When in the bloody hell had that happened?

However, I knew. It had begun on the Isle of Crete...

Since he was not here— where the devil was he anyway? — there was obviously no point building a fire at the stove.

Instead, I turned on the electric light at the desk, then went to the chalkboard and entered the most recent notes in the

Bennett inquiry case, along with a note— in the event that Brodie returned —that I would next be contacting Dr. Pennington at Oxford. Along with a mental reminder to inquire about a copy of Dr. Bennett's book.

It would undoubtedly be dry reading, medical procedures and all that, however it might provide some insight into the man.

Having made my notes I glanced at the clock on the wall. It was very near five o'clock in the evening, a reminder that I had promised Lily that we would attend Templeton's newest performance at Drury Lane in Covent Garden.

Curtain time was for eight o'clock. That gave me just enough time to return to Mayfair for a change of clothes, and perhaps an early supper with Lily.

I placed a call to Sussex Square. My sister eventually picked up the call. She was quite out of breath and laughing.

"Theater?" she echoed my invitation. "I would love to attend." And my earlier plans were suddenly changed.

"And our aunt as well. We will meet you there," she informed me. That was certainly quite different for my sister. She was inclined toward opera, the long, often boring, Italian sort. An evening at Drury Lane was most out of character for her.

It seemed that Mr. Warren would be joining us as well, which spoke volumes about what she insisted was a non-relationship. They were "merely friends" of course, though no one believed it for a moment considering her unexplained and frequent absences when not overseeing Lily's artistic endeavors.

Most interesting, I thought. It was also an opportunity to inquire if Mr. Warren might be able to acquire a copy of Dr. Bennett's book for me.

"That will give us sufficient time to clean ourselves of paint and dress," Linnie continued.

It seemed that she had spent the afternoon assisting Lily with different mediums of art— oil paintings and watercolors as well.

"The solar has excellent light however the windows are quite covered with paint."

I could only imagine how that might have happened.

"Lily really does have an amazing memory for things. She completely memorized all the prints in my old school portfolio and can readily describe the differences between Cézanne and Van Gogh and explain their techniques."

There was more of course, as there usually was when it came to my sister's passion for art.

"First curtain is at eight o'clock," I reminded her.

"Will Mr. Brodie be joining us, as well?" she asked.

I returned to Mayfair to prepare for the evening at the theater. There was still no word from Brodie. Aggravating man.

"Will Mr. Brodie be joining you for an early supper and the theater?" Mrs. Ryan inquired.

"He's off on some matter of business," I replied, with absolutely no idea what that was.

I thought this was no way to begin this new part of our relationship, him off on his own, myself left to my own devices — which was quite a revelation since I had never before cared a fig how a man, any man, might conduct himself. And the same for me as well as I was not of the habit of explaining myself to anyone.

Hmmm. Most interesting.

"Very well, I will serve supper for yourself, then." She turned toward the dining room and the adjacent kitchen.

"Not a way to start a marriage to my way of thinkin'."

Never let it be said that Mrs. Ryan was shy about expressing an opinion.

After an early supper, I dressed with only a couple of remarks from her.

I distracted her from further comments when I asked her to call for a cab. The truth was, I had no previous experience regarding marriage other than the examples set by my father— not the best example of a loving relationship. Then there was my sister's marriage that had ended badly. Wasn't there a man who honored that commitment?

That little voice told me there most certainly was, however, he was off chasing down some matter for Sir Avery. Of course. That had to be it. Then again, what if something had happened to him?

I frowned as I pushed back that thought. Brodie knew well enough how to take care of himself.

The evening at the theater was to be a family affair, or as close to family as the five of us— my sister, our great-aunt, myself, and now Lily might be.

It was Templeton's opening night, and our aunt was quite excited about it.

I had just arrived at the theater entrance separately and left the hired coach when I heard Lily call out. I wouldn't have recognized her if she hadn't run toward me quite excited in that way of hers since arriving in London.

She wore a long gown and someone— my sister undoubtedly —had fixed her hair, coiled and then anchored at the back of her head. Her eyes gleamed with excitement as she seized both my hands.

"I never seen anything like this!" she exclaimed. I braced myself for a list of things *"she had never seen before."* It was exciting to see things through her eyes.

"Look at all the ladies and gents," she continued on. "Everyone in their finest. The only time I ever seen such finery was the gents when they came to the Church for the evening."

"Church?" my aunt commented as she joined us.

There were a few things I had decided not to explain about Lily's background for now. The "Church" that had been converted into a brothel was one of those things.

And then true to her nature, our aunt was off on another topic.

"I've heard it's quite a holiday production, a musical, and not one of those boring pieces by Shakespeare. Templeton does seem to have a preference for those. I cannot imagine the reason."

If she only knew, I thought, and wondered what Mr. Shakespeare might have to say about this new production, and if he would put in an appearance— spiritually speaking of course —as he did have a way of popping in from time to time according to Templeton.

Lily's excited chatter continued on about the lights all about the entrance to the theater, the life-size playbill that featured an image of Templeton in full costume for the play. And then there was the statue in the foyer of the theater— the life-size statue of Mr. Shakespeare himself.

"Crivvens!" she exclaimed, a favorite word I had heard a great deal of lately. "What is that?"

"That is a statue of William Shakespeare, a very famous playwright," Linnie explained. "Templeton has performed in several of his plays."

"He looks like he has a complaint of the bowel." Lily commented.

I choked back laughter.

From what Templeton had shared in the past, Mr. Shakespeare was not fond of the statue either. I did hope he didn't take offense at Lily's observation.

"Good evening, Miss Forsythe and Miss Lenore."

I recognized that voice from our previous encounter at Hatchards book shop. As I turned, Sir James Redstone nodded in greeting.

"And Lady Montgomery. So very good to see you once again. It has been a while."

I caught the slight lift of one of my aunt's eyebrows. For her part, it seemed as if a dark cloud had settled over Lily considering the frown on her face.

"Sir James," my aunt greeted him. "It has been some time. Before your last journey to the Orient, as I remember, that has kept you away from London."

"There are many fascinating things to see and learn from other places. Wouldn't you agree, Miss Forsythe?" The comment obviously for me.

"That's Mrs. Brodie." Lily commented from under that dark cloud which brought a stern exclamation from my sister, however I found it most amusing.

"Lily has recently joined our family," Linnie went on to explain.

"Ah, a charity endeavor," Redstone concluded.

"I am grateful, if it's anythin' to ye," Lily bluntly replied.

I decided that it was time to intervene.

"Templeton asked that we call on her in her dressing room before the performance," I announced. "It is very near that time. We should be going."

"Perhaps you would like to join me in my box," I overheard Redstone say to my aunt.

It was very gracious of him, however, my aunt had a box at the theater next to the royal box out of deference to her family, history, and long-standing support of the theater.

"You must join us," she replied. "And you must tell me all about your latest travels. I am planning on going on safari the coming year. Have you been?"

And they were off to our aunt's theater box, including my sister. Lily hung back, that dark expression still on her face, and in spite of my resolve not to do so, I found myself telling her something I was once told.

"Your face will freeze like that."

She angled that dark blue gaze at me. "I dinnae like the man."

"You don't know him. He's quite well known and respected."

"I know others like him. I seen 'em at the 'Church' and on the streets. They say one thing to yer face, then do another behind yer back. Madame always said, get the coin up front or ye won't get it at all."

Quite an observation for one so young.

"Her ladyship can take care of herself," I assured her.

"Like you, Mr. Brodie told me?"

I knew well enough where Templeton's dressing room was from previous performances at the theater, and informed the attendant as Lily and I made our way through a door that led to the backstage and dressing room area.

"Ye might want to be careful, miss," he cautioned,

although he didn't indicate what the reason might be other than the usual moving around of props by backstage attendants and the usual bustle of performers before the play began.

However, I didn't have long to wonder at his comment as we traversed the area at the back of the stage and I heard a faint swishing sound amid other sounds one usually found behind the scenes.

I laid a hand on Lily's arm as we neared Templeton's dressing room. I heard it again, louder and very distinct. I knew that sound along with the curse from a stagehand that usually followed.

"Crivvens!" Lily exclaimed. "A dragon!"

I had the same thought, as I stepped in front of her and the "dragon." More precisely, Ziggy. However, she was not the least bit frightened, merely curious.

"He's an iguana," I replied. "From South America. He's a pet and quite harmless," I explained, and it appeared to have returned from the London Zoo where he had been residing the past several months.

As I said, she wasn't the least bit frightened.

"Wot's he doing here?" Lily asked.

"He's an escape artist," Templeton explained, as she attempted to guide Ziggy in the direction of her dressing room. No mean feat as he looked at her with beady eyes and hissed. He obviously was not of the same opinion about returning there.

My friend was dressed for her performance, complete with makeup, and a sprig of holly adorning her hair.

I wasn't certain if Lily had ever been to the theater. This evening apparently was going to be full of new experiences, Ziggy included.

Lily had emerged from behind me and approached Ziggy as if he was someone's pet dog.

"Wot does he eat?"

"Plants for the most part," Templeton replied. "He's particularly fond of roses."

And there were at least a dozen more questions.

"And you are?" Templeton then asked.

However, before introductions were made, "Oh my!" my friend exclaimed. "I'm getting something…" Her fingers were pressed against her temple in a way I had seen before.

"You are quite gifted, my dear," she told Lily. She smiled. "Wills says that you have an incredible memory for things. Oh, and the dead rat you put in a particular gentleman's coat pocket was most effective."

I looked at Lily. A dead rat?

"He deserved it," she explained as she patted Ziggy on the head. As I said, much like a pet dog.

"He tried to put his hands up my skirt at the place Madame set up shop until she could find a more proper place after the Church burned down. I used the knife on him wot Munro gave me before ye left Old Town. He said it could be useful."

Indeed.

"The man was a rat. And I found one in the kitchen at the place Madame rented. So I thought to send him a message next time he came round to visit one of the ladies."

"Oh, my," Templeton exclaimed. "It seems you're quite the adventuress." She wrapped an arm around Lily's shoulders.

"It is so very good to meet you," she told Lily with an amused glance at me.

She handed the roses to Lily. "Hold this in front of Ziggy. As I said he's particularly partial to roses. Poor thing. He had lost a great deal of his color whilst at the zoo, and had become quite lonely," she said, then led the way back to her dressing room.

Lily and Ziggy followed.

Adventuress, I thought? And what was that about an incredible memory?

To say that Lily was fascinated with Ziggy and Templeton was another one of those understatements. He looked much the same as I remembered. As for being lonely, I did wonder how one might know.

Did an iguana sit over in a corner with a sad expression, perhaps refusing to eat?

"And where is Mr. Brodie?" Templeton inquired as Elvira Finch put the finishing touches to her makeup.

At present Ziggy was laying at Lily's feet, quite content after consuming a full bouquet of roses.

"He's making inquiries in a new case," I explained since the inquiries on Sir Avery's behalf were usually of a most secretive nature.

"And...?" she added with a glance at my reflection in the mirror before her. She looked quite festive.

"I've been pursuing a separate matter for a client."

"And...?" she repeated. "What of your new arrangement with Mr. Brodie?"

It could hardly be said that Brodie and I had a conventional relationship. The truth was, I thought with faint irritation, that I didn't have a clue what our relationship was supposed to be now.

It wasn't as if I was home cooking and cleaning and waiting supper for him to return for the evening. I didn't even know where our home was, between the room adjacent to the office and my townhouse in Mayfair.

I finally replied, "He's quite busy, and I have an inquiry

case as well."

I caught the look she gave me. I did hope she wasn't receiving a message from Wills in the matter. Her ability to communicate with the man was going to be difficult enough to explain to Lily as it was.

There was a knock on her dressing room door and an attendant popped his head inside and announced that it was very near curtain call time.

"Wot about Ziggy?" Lily asked.

Ziggy was at present apparently quite content, eyes closed, sprawled in front of Lily.

"He'll be all right," Templeton replied. "I have to keep him in the dressing room. He has a habit of wanting to join the production. It can cause quite a stir among the other actors and patrons."

An understatement to be certain. Ziggy's previous foray about the theater during a play had caused an uproar that had managed to empty the place.

Lily thoroughly enjoyed the play with unbridled enthusiasm, often leaning out over the balustrade of my aunt's box for a better view. Much of course, to Sir James Redstone's obvious disapproval.

She couldn't have cared less, and I was in complete agreement.

The play was a complete success and Templeton invited us to join her for a late supper at the Savoy afterward.

Sir James accepted. He had been most attentive to my aunt throughout the evening. She laughed and flirted a bit, something surprising as she was not usually given to such things.

However, I supposed at her age, she was allowed to do just about anything. I declined the invitation, much to my sister's disappointment.

"The recent changes at the Savoy are said to be quite spectacular," she said in an effort to persuade me to attend.

"Everyone has been talking about how difficult it is to get a table. You must go."

I must not, I thought. I wasn't impressed by elaborate dining rooms or exclusive table reservations. I would much rather have shared a late supper with Brodie at the Strand. And then, of course, a dram afterward.

That surprised me and I wondered when that had happened.

"I don't want to go," Lily whispered to me. "I don't like him."

Since Sir James was the only male present, it seemed obvious who she was referring to.

"You don't know him," I pointed out.

"I know others like him," she replied. "They put on fine clothes and speak fancy words. But underneath all the finery that's not who they really are. I seen a lot of that."

I supposed that came from the past several years working in a brothel in Edinburgh. We had both seen a great deal in our escape the night of the fire.

She looked up at me. "I want to go with ye."

I had planned to return to the office once more after the theater, in the event that Brodie might have returned. There was certainly no reason that she couldn't accompany me there on our way to Mayfair. I congratulated Templeton on a splendid opening night and we departed.

Outside the theater, Drury Lane and the adjacent streets were jammed with coaches, those who had attended the play, and late evening street vendors that also included a young man selling ice cream from a cart.

"I ain't never... I never had such," Lily corrected herself. "The best we ever had at Madame's was pudding if it was left over once the gents left the morning after their visit."

She did have a colorful way of describing things. The vendor was quite obviously Italian by his accent and his compliments to Lily.

"Bellissima," he praised her as he handed her frozen raspberry ice cream in a wafer cup.

Her eyes were like two saucers on her face. It was worth two pennies to see the reaction.

"Crivvens!" she exclaimed. "This is better than day old pudding."

I certainly agreed with her as I ordered one as well, and we walked about the lane with bright lights and ice cream, Lily chattering on about the play, Templeton, and Ziggy.

It had been quite an evening for her, and a bit of an adventure for me as well.

Late as it was, we found a cab, and Lily returned with me to Mayfair after stopping briefly at the office. She was still chattering about the play when Mrs. Ryan met us at the door.

"Are there any messages?" I asked as I removed my coat and hat.

There weren't any.

The only other time there was no contact from Brodie, he had taken himself off to Edinburgh. At the time, I had been prepared for it to be several days or more considering the reason.

I was to go to Oxford the next day and meet with Dr. Pennington. Granted, Brodie would have found Oxford, with thirty schools spread across the entire campus, to be tedious in the least.

I would carry on, on behalf of Mrs. Bennett, on my own as I had the last several days.

I did hope that Dr. Pennington might be able to provide some insight into Dr. Bennett's habits, and where he might have taken himself off to.

I followed Lily into the parlor where Mrs. Ryan had a fire going upon the hearth. She was finally winding down much like a top that had spun itself out, as my aunt had once said of me.

Mrs. Ryan provided hot cocoa; another wondrous thing Lily knew about but had never experienced.

"Ice cream and hot chocolate all in one evening?" Mrs. Ryan commented as I poured a bit of Old Lodge whisky.

"You'll spoil the child."

I smiled. "I certainly hope so."

Two cups of hot cocoa and the "child" was quite drowsy. I accompanied her upstairs to the guest bedroom.

"Thank ye kindly, miss," she said around a yawn. "I ain't never had nothin' like tonight."

We hadn't quite worked out what she was supposed to call me. *Mother* seemed inappropriate since I was very definitely not her mother. *Miss Forsythe* was too formal as if the arrangement was only temporary. And I didn't care for *Lady Forsythe*. Again, it was far too formal and seemed to emphasize where I came from even though I had never cared a fig about titles... and had a way of putting distance between people as I knew only too well.

She slipped out of the gown, then unknotted her hair in front of the dressing table mirror. I caught the gesture as she ran her fingers over the brush that lay atop the dresser.

"I ain't never had such fine things, miss— the clothes, this room, and this." She ran her fingers across the soft bristles. "'Course there are the lessons, art, and music that Miss Lenore says every proper young girl should have."

That did sound like my sister.

I picked the brush up and ran it through her hair, gently removing the twists and coils.

An old memory— which I rarely allowed —suddenly came back to me.

Our mother had died when Linnie and I were very young. After we went to live at Sussex Square there were maids and other servants, and most certainly our great-aunt to see to our needs. And there had been great affection as well.

Tonight I had taken on the part that our mother might have shared with us... brushing our hair, telling us stories, taking us for ice cream in a wafer cup after a play.

We hadn't had that. I pushed the memory back where it belonged, in the past.

"Miss?"

I hadn't realized that I had stopped brushing her hair. I caught Lily's reflection in the mirror above the dressing table.

"I've been thinking," I told her.

Brodie would certainly have made a comment at that, or perhaps narrowed that dark gaze as he was quite familiar with such words when I had an idea that I wanted to share.

"I have a name. It's quite all right for you to use it. Now, off with you to bed. It's very late."

"Good night, miss..." she said sleepily from under the down comforter, then before drifting off, "Mikaela. It was a right splendid day, weren't it?" There was a yawn that followed.

"Yes, it was."

The only thing missing in all of this was Brodie.

## Six

I RECEIVED a message from Mr. Brimley in the morning. He had spoken with Dr. Pennington, who was currently providing a lecture series at the medical school at Oxford, regarding my inquiries into Dr. Bennett.

Dr. Pennington had provided valuable information in a previous inquiry case. Although his schedule was quite fractured, as he had put it, he would be more than pleased to meet with me if I was agreeable to come to Oxford.

I rose early to find Lily was already awake and downstairs, chatting away with Mrs. Ryan. In a short amount of time the two of them had become thick as thieves as the saying went.

Mrs. Ryan seemed particularly taken with Lily. I took that as a good sign as my friend Templeton would have said, after the horrible circumstances over the death of her daughter, Mary.

"Lily has been telling me all about the play at the Drury," my housekeeper commented as I joined them. "And ice cream after? It's a wonder the girl didn't end up with a misery of the stomach."

Lily merely grinned.

I had thought that it might be another adventure for her to accompany me to Oxford, however that was put aside for another time when my sister rang up.

She had made arrangements for Lily to accompany her to Sotheby's and the auction of various pieces of Egyptian artifacts and statues they were hosting.

When I explained to Lily, she had made a face.

"I first attended Sotheby's when I was very near your age," I consoled her. "You will find many fascinating things there. I'm certain that it led to my first adventure." I forced myself to keep a straight face at her response to that.

"I seen some drawings that Lady Antonia had in her art room. Masks of dead people and bodies in boxes?"

That was rather cutting to the heart of it.

"Ancient kings and queens," I replied in an attempt to pique her curiosity. "And undoubtedly a well-preserved snake or a ram covered in gold."

That brought about a disapproving sound from Mrs. Ryan. However, it had the desired effect.

"A sheep covered in gold?"

"The ram represented the ancient god, Amun. The sign of the ram or a goat's head has been found on the walls of many tombs. That would be far more interesting than an afternoon at Oxford."

"A sheep covered in gold?"

I had read about that in the dailies, promoting the exhibition and auction.

She seemed to be considering that as opposed to Oxford which I had explained was actually several schools located in the town of Oxford.

"Over thirty schools at one place?" she exclaimed as I explained that Oxford was actually a combination of many different colleges, including the women's college that had opened in 1879.

"Wot does anyone need with that many schools? Ye'd die before ye learnt it all."

She did have a very pragmatic way of thinking that I couldn't argue with.

"I s'pose I'd rather see a gold sheep than all those schools," she finally decided.

"Although I'd much rather go with ye in yer new investigation."

With that more or less agreed upon, I had Mrs. Ryan make arrangements for my aunt's driver to pick Lily up for her return to Sussex Square, which brought me around to the subject of Rupert.

He had joined us once more the previous evening when we went by the office on the Strand, in keeping with Brodie's instructions to Mr. Cavendish. He insisted that the hound accompany Lily and I to Mayfair.

This morning Rupert was presently reclined before the hearth in the front parlor with only an occasional twitch to give any indication that he was still alive.

I would be making the trip to Oxford by way of Paddington Rail Station and while it was possible that I might take him along, I did foresee some objections from the attendants not to mention other passengers.

He did have a way of putting people off somewhat if not with his over-protective manner, then most certainly by the smell that accompanied him when he'd been out and about the streets.

"I'll see that he gets to Mr. Cavendish then accompany Lily

to Sussex Square," Mrs. Ryan spoke up as I considered precisely what was to be done.

I looked over in surprise. It was one thing that she provided biscuits and scones for Mr. Cavendish and Rupert. It was quite another to go about London with the hound in a coach much like a favored pet.

"There's no need to look at me like that," she commented. "It will give me the opportunity to air the place after ye're on yer way and the girl is quite fond of him."

Lily grinned.

Oxford was more than an hour away by rail.

When I rang up Dr. Pennington's office, his assistant informed me that the doctor suggested that we meet at an inn, rather than negotiating the vast grounds and halls of the medical school.

Oxford University was known across the empire and the rest of the world as one of the premier universities. The original school dated back almost to the time of the Norman Conquest with records that went back as far as the year 1096.

"*Your several generations great-uncle studied there, something near very eight hundred years ago,*" my great-aunt had shared with my sister and me with a casual wave of her hand.

"*It's all there in our library, of course. Quite boring,*" she had added.

This was according to her grandfather who kept family records of such things. It was also where our father had studied. Not that it spoke well of his character.

The Chequers Inn was on High Street in Oxford. It had originally been a coaching inn for travelers to and from

London, and then a meeting place for students and professors from the university.

It was a plaster and stone two-story building with meeting rooms over the tavern on the main floor. There were dark wood beams and a serving bar with fireplaces that kept it warm after the chill of the ride from the station, and had undoubtedly warmed a fair share of highwaymen lifting a pint after lifting a purse or two on the road.

I would have appreciated a bit of Old Lodge to warm myself, but ordered a cup of coffee instead. I explained that Dr. Pennington would be joining me. The man behind the bar, by the name of Alfie, nodded.

"Know 'im well. He meets regular with some of the others upstairs when he's over from London for a lecture."

Dr. Pennington arrived a short time later, stamping his boots at the entrance with the snow that had begun.

He was of medium height with close cropped dark hair and beard just beginning to gray about the edges. Not a particularly handsome man, he had a scholarly appearance as if his thoughts were chasing a dozen different things at one time.

Alfie greeted him with a gesture in my direction, and Dr. Pennington looked up and smiled.

He had provided information in a previous inquiry case on behalf of Mr. Brimley that had been most important. Dr. Bennett was an acquaintance as well as an associate at St. James Hospital according to Mr. Brimley, and I hoped he might be able to provide some insight into Dr. Bennett's recent disappearance.

He greeted me with the familiarity of that past case. "A bit brisk out today," he commented.

Brisk. Now there was a word, I thought, as my hands had just begun to thaw by way of the coffee mug.

Dr. Pennington was most congenial, not all the stuffy colle-
giate sort that I was most familiar with, and curious what I had
been up to as he put it.

"And her ladyship?" he inquired as we exchanged pleas-
antries.

Was there anyone who didn't know my great-aunt?

I assured him that she was quite well and fully recovered
from the injury to her ankle.

"And how is my good friend?" he inquired of Mr. Brimley.

I assured him that he was quite well, and deeply involved
with a new specimen he had acquired.

"The man is quite brilliant," he replied. "A tragedy that he
could not complete his studies. However, I admire the choice
he made and his care for others."

The barkeep served him coffee as well. He took a long sip of
the steaming brew.

"I would normally have Alfie add a bit of extra warmth," he
said with obvious meaning. "However, I have a late afternoon
lecture and then a meeting with the chairman of the medical
school.

"Now, my dear Miss Forsythe, what has brought you to
Oxford? Another inquiry case? How may I be of assistance?"

I explained the circumstances of the inquiry; Mrs.
Bennett's initial contact over a month earlier and then further
concerns more recently.

"Ah, my colleague in medicine. Yes, I know Dr. Bennett
from our university days. He was a full year ahead of myself.
Quite exceptional actually, and very much interested in
experimental techniques. He was greatly affected by the loss
of a younger brother who had a commission with the
military.

"The young man was severely injured in a dreadful

encounter in the Sudan, as I remember. He returned while we were at university, however, was horribly scarred and maimed."

He leaned in close. "Took his own life, unable to live with the situation. Terrible tragedy that effected Joseph deeply according to others who knew him as well.

"It was after that terrible situation that he left Oxford and went to France for a time. He studied there about certain restorative procedures for injuries such as his brother had. That seemed to motivate him. He returned to Oxford and finished his studies then began his apprenticeship."

By everything he told me, it seemed that Dr. Bennett was successful as well as brilliant.

"Successful, yes. Quite so to all outward appearances. However, having experienced it myself, he spoke more than once that those of our profession were slow to accept new practices that were not new at all according to what he had learned while in France."

"What might those have been?" I asked.

"Ways of restoring the use of limbs with intricate surgery, as well as helping those who had suffered burns. He was most fascinated by records discovered in Egypt about ancient procedures to repair facial features as well as surgeries of the brain. The Egyptians were quite advanced in those things."

I then asked him if he had noticed any recent changes in Dr. Bennett. For some it would have been a delicate matter— a wife's inquiries about absences, then not returning at all the past three nights.

"If you are inquiring as to whether or not there might have been another woman, or perhaps something else that occupied his time, my response would be no. He is not the sort."

As opposed to a man who would be the sort?

He was thoughtful. "I do hold you and your efforts in high

esteem, Miss Forsythe. You seem a woman of common sense and not given to rash behavior."

I accepted that as a compliment, odd as it seemed.

"In the past you have conducted yourself with discretion."

If not the possibility of another woman and an affair, I did wonder where this was leading.

"Joseph has spoken often about the need to follow certain techniques outside the usual boundaries of our fellow gentlemen in medicine. To that end, he indicated that he needed a place apart from St. James and the established medical profession.

"He seemed to be of a mind to work independently to establish the practices that he had discovered in his time away from Oxford."

"When was this?"

"He first mentioned it upon his return. However, more recently he has been absent from the hospital and taken fewer patients."

More recently turned out to be the past six months.

"It is possible that he set up a private practice apart from St. James," he commented.

When he had the occasion to ask Dr. Bennett about those absences, he had only provided a vague response.

"He said that his wife was having some health issues. However, now with your inquiry, it is even more puzzling."

Puzzling indeed. Mrs. Bennett seemed quite healthy when last we met. Most interesting.

We shared a lunch at the inn. Dr. Pennington was then expected back for his afternoon lecture.

"I do hope nothing serious has happened," he said in parting. "As I said, the man is brilliant and I greatly miss our conversations. You will let me know once you've resolved your inquiry?"

I assured him that I would. I then returned to the rail station to await the next return train to London.

Dr. Pennington had been extremely complimentary of Dr. Bennett. Quite brilliant he had called him, and deeply affected by the loss of his younger brother. So much so that he had sought out medical treatments that might have made a difference had he known about them earlier.

It wasn't unusual that a tragedy set someone on a particular course in life. On the one hand, as Brodie would say, the man was to be commended for pursuing something that would make a difference to others in the future. On the other hand, there was the fact that Dr. Bennett was now apparently among the missing.

What did it mean?

Was it possible he had taken himself off, as Dr. Pennington explained, to pursue private practice that might provide him the freedom to apply the things he had learned? If so, then what reason was there for him to simply disappear?

Surely he could pursue those aspects of his profession in private. Couldn't he? And where might that be?

A private office to be certain, some place discreet and away from those who would have been critical of his techniques?

Where to begin?

I was going to need assistance with this, from someone who knew the streets of London, had lived on them and had connections where others might not. Quite naturally Brodie came to mind, however, I already had my answer there. He had made it very clear that I could pursue this on my own.

Very well, I thought as my train pulled into Paddington

Station, I would pursue this. After all, we had a client who was very much in need of answers.

I knew the best person to assist me. He could be a bit difficult in such matters, no doubt owing to his loyalty to Brodie. However, I was certain he could be persuaded. He simply needed to see it as assisting me so that I was not going off on this alone, and he had proven to be most capable of assisting in the past. In fact, Brodie frequently relied upon him for information on one matter or another when making inquiries.

Perfect, I thought.

"No!" Munro replied most emphatically when I explained the situation and what needed to be explored next.

I had heard that before, in stronger language from another stubborn Scot.

"Very well, then I shall acquire Mr. Dooley's services in the matter." That brought the response I thought it might.

"Dooley? The man is competent as far as it goes, and I know he's been of assistance in the past. But he dinnae know everything that goes on out on the street."

I had learned over the past two years that there was a way of knowing precisely when I had persuaded one with my argument.

"He'd not approve of yer doin' this," he pointed out, obviously referring to Brodie.

I set aside my immediate response to the fact that I didn't need anyone's approval, in favor of seizing the moment as I heard Munro hesitate.

"Mrs. Bennett is quite concerned that something has happened to Dr. Bennett," I continued.

"And Brodie would undoubtedly not approve of your sending me off alone. When can you begin your inquiries?"

There was a round of curses that reached all the way from the wine cellar below the main floor at Sussex Square where I had sought him, up to the kitchens on the main floor.

Two of my aunt's maids and the cook looked at me with startled expressions as I emerged from the wine cellar. I merely smiled.

Angus Brodie swore at the information Alex Sinclair had picked up from one of the Agency contacts in Brussels and now handed to him.

"How old is this information?"

"No more than a few hours. Communication can sometimes be garbled coming in across the channel. And then it took a bit longer to clarify it."

"Has Sir Avery seen this?"

"Not yet," Alex replied. "I wanted to be certain of it, before I took it to him."

"Is it reliable?" Brodie asked.

"The man who intercepted it has been reliable in the past..." Alex hesitated. "Then the communication ended. We've been unable to reach him since to verify."

The first message and one other had been intercepted as well, some weeks earlier indicating that the man, Soropkin, was to meet with someone in London who could help their cause.

But precisely what was that cause, Brodie thought? And where was Soropkin now?

He had been chasing down bits and pieces of information

since returning with Mikaela from Scotland and had contacted Herr Schmidt at the German Gymnasium.

The man had previously assisted in a particular matter and seemed to have an ear to the ground, so to speak. He seemed to know just about everything that went on in the immigrant communities in the East End. Both legal and illegal.

Brodie wouldn't have called him a friend, but the man had proven to be reliable when it concerned matters in that community that could be most serious and have far reaching repercussions.

When the first information surfaced in that early communication, he had gone to Schmidt for any gossip that might have been picked up on the streets.

It was always a tricky matter dealing with the different immigrant communities in the East End as he knew only too well from his time with the MET. The Germans didn't trust the Russians. The Russians felt likewise and had no love for those from Poland or any of the other European countries.

And then there was the mutual suspicion of those from beyond Europe, and some of the places Mikaela had traveled on her adventures. It was like a pot that could boil over at any time as each established their own areas and guarded them fiercely.

Someone might arrive and then simply disappear in the East End, without being noticed. But with this intercepted message, it seemed that Soropkin's people had managed to slip into the country. Those earlier rumblings that had been merely rumors at the time about something that was planned, were apparently far more concrete now.

He needed to contact Schmidt again. Soropkin was responsible for the deaths of dozens of persons in Germany and there was most certainly no love lost there. With this, it was possible that Schmidt or one of his people might know something about this latest communication.

"Make certain that Sir Avery sees this right away," he told Alex as he grabbed the revolver he carried and checked it, then grabbed his long coat.

"I'll be out and about for a while to see what other information there might be," he added.

That was as much as he was willing to reveal for now. He'd lived on the streets in the past and valued the trust Schmidt had in him, so far.

That went both ways. He kept the names of those he relied on to himself. Nothing was written down, no names mentioned, nor put into one of those reports that Sir Avery submitted to others. Not even to Alex, even though he trusted the young man.

But, as he'd also learned on the streets, the walls had ears. What one man overheard and might pass on, at least a dozen more might learn of, and he wouldn't put any man at risk.

It was precisely the reason he was determined to keep Mikaela out of this. Not that she couldn't be trusted. He'd never known a woman who wasna given to gossip, until she boldly walked into his life.

Quite the opposite and it was precisely that reason that he had kept the details of this from her. It would be just like her, once she heard what they'd learned, to insist on being part of it.

Not this time, he thought, not now, as he buttoned his coat and set off to find a driver to take him back to the office on the Strand to change into clothes far more suitable for where he was going next.

He needed to go back to the streets, blend in, move about without suspicion, and see what he could learn.

# Seven

AFTER MEETING WITH DR. PENNINGTON, I
did have more questions for Mrs. Bennett. It did seem that
there were things she might have overlooked or had chosen not
to mention regarding Dr. Bennett's work. There might be
nothing at all or it might provide something important.

I had then returned to the office on the Strand after
enlisting the somewhat reluctant assistance of Munro the
previous afternoon. Once again, there was no sign of Brodie.
Not that I was concerned, or the sort who went on and on
about such things...

Mr. Cavendish insisted the hound accompany me to the
townhouse upon my leaving. Mrs. Ryan had returned with the
hound on her way to Sussex Square the previous day. He had
somehow terrorized a neighbor who lived next to the townhouse as the man went to collect the daily. When I learned who
it was, a curmudgeonly sort I had encountered on more than
one occasion, I thought Rupert should be congratulated.

So there we were, Rupert and myself at the townhouse. I
set the fire on the hearth in the front parlor, poured myself a bit

of Old Lodge, and then found something for both of us to eat in the cold box in the kitchen. After supper, I had placed a call to Mrs. Bennett and arranged to meet this morning.

It was quite late when I finally retired for the night, Rupert accompanying me upstairs, and I contemplated the situation with Brodie.

Such things did have a way of creeping into one's thoughts when one had a dram or two.

I could only surmise what his work for Sir Avery might be. He had shown a particular displeasure toward the man in the last case that had taken us to Edinburgh, a personal matter that Brodie needed to resolve. And I was aware that it was not the first time there was a difference of opinions in certain matters between the two men.

And there was the other part of it and quite surprising... I missed him. I missed our conversations at the end of the day. I even missed our occasional disagreements over a certain matter. Such things had never bothered me before. And there was that other part of our relationship now.

It did occur to me that with recent events, pathetic as it was, I did lament that the only creature in my bed— or beside it on the floor, was the hound. The smell about him was far different from the scent of cinnamon about Brodie.

Oh, bloody hell.

The hounded sounded off as the bell at the door rang upon the arrival of the driver for my meeting with Mrs. Bennett.

I collected my coat, then gathered my umbrella along with the bag that contained my notebook. I gave the hound a long look.

It was undoubtedly not a good idea to simply leave him at the townhouse with no one about. I could only imagine what I might find upon my return.

The alternative was to simply turn him out. However, there was my neighbor to consider. I have to admit that it was tempting, however I didn't want any harm to come to the hound over the matter.

"Oh very well, do come along," I told him, and made certain that I had several of Mrs. Ryan's biscuits in hand as we departed.

A little persuasion couldn't hurt... That brought my thoughts back round to Brodie. Irritating man.

I sat in the front parlor of the Bennett residence at Belgrave Square, and politely accepted the tea the housekeeper had served.

"Is there any word?" Mrs. Bennett anxiously asked when we were once more alone.

"I'm afraid not," I replied.

She had not heard from him as well nor had he returned. Her previously calm manner was betrayed by the shaking of her hand as she set her own cup back on the saucer with a clatter.

She abruptly rose as if she could not bear to simply sit, and began to pace across the floor, a handkerchief clutched in one hand.

"There have been late evenings with his work, however he has never failed to return home. He is so very dedicated," she went on to explain then wiped at the tears that came.

She was obviously quite distraught and very near the edge. However, after my conversation with Dr. Pennington, I did have additional questions. As I knew all too well from our inquiry cases, very often there were things that a wife might not be fully aware of but might suspect.

"I have learned some things that might be useful, with your help," I continued.

"Yes, of course!" She turned. "Anything that I can do..."

She sat once more at the edge of the chair across from me. I didn't go into perhaps the more obvious reason that Dr. Bennett might not have returned the past three days after a pattern of late nights the past several weeks.

There was the possibility of gambling, which was a pastime for some. God knows my own father had the habit. I mentioned it as delicately as possible, even though I was well aware that one's wife was often the last to know of such things.

She shook her head. "I manage our household expenses My brother is head clerk at the bank. If there were any..." she chose her words carefully, "irregularities, I would know of it."

The next question was far more delicate, however it needed to be asked. I chose my words carefully.

"Has there ever been any estrangement in the past?"

"Estrangement? Are you asking if my husband has ever had a relationship with another woman?" she inquired.

"It is something that is known to happen..."

"No," she replied quite adamantly, then seemed to gather herself once more. "My husband is a brilliant man..." she continued, and I wondered if it was an attempt to convince me or herself. "He has devoted himself completely to his profession. It is everything to him, particularly after the death of his brother some years ago. Do you understand, Miss Forsythe?"

I did understand but didn't go into it— the things that made each of us who we were.

There was another possibility, of course, that the doctor had met with some misfortune.

I explained that I had met with Dr. Pennington and that there seemed to be some dissatisfaction on Dr. Bennett's part regarding the Medical Society and criticism he had received in the past. I noted the way her gaze slipped away from mine, her hands twisting in her lap.

"The Society hasn't always valued his work. There were... letters that he received that upset him greatly."

"What sort of letters?"

"At first they were from colleagues he worked with— two of them. Then another from the chairman of King's College where he attended and has also lectured."

"Do you have those letters?"

She shook her head. "I saw only one. He kept the others to himself, although they bothered him enormously."

"Kept at a private office perhaps?" I suggested.

She shook her head. "Oh, he didn't keep a private office away from the hospital. I do know that he was greatly frustrated by certain... expectations of the Medical Society and at the hospital. He commented more than once that what they supported in many cases was no more than butchery that left people maimed afterward."

I thought of a young officer Brodie and I had met during a previous inquiry case, badly injured in the Sudan. However, he had sufficiently recovered, although he would always carry an obvious limp from the injury.

"Might I see the letter you have?" I asked. There might be something there that could provide better insight.

She rose from the chair and went to a side table that sat before bookshelves on one wall. She opened the drawer and took out an envelope, then handed it to me.

"If it might help," she said.

I pulled the letter from the envelope. It was written on official stationery and was dated very near six months earlier. It was a formal reprimand and stated that if there were further "questionable" actions, an official inquiry would be made.

There was the usual blather about it being regrettable that the letter was necessary given Dr. Bennett's dedication and skill, much in need by those of his profession. And the mention of a particularly difficult case he had taken on with a successful outcome for a prominent member of Parliament.

However, the tone was obvious. It was a warning that other such *activities* would not be tolerated.

I folded the letter and returned it to the envelope.

"Did Dr. Bennett explain what those other activities might be?" I asked since it seemed possible that it might have something to do with recent events.

"He didn't discuss the specifics of his cases with me," Mrs. Bennett replied. "However I do know that he was frustrated by what he referred to as antiquated practices that often left someone maimed from an injury when additional care might have prevented a patient from losing a limb."

I thought of Mr. Cavendish who maneuvered about incredibly well considering his previous injuries that had resulted in the loss of both legs. However I did wonder what new treatments might now be done for such wounds that would restore the use of the legs or arms.

What more did this tell me about Dr. Bennett?

That he was devoted to his profession, driven by the tragic loss of his brother, perhaps brilliant as his wife insisted, and then frustrated by the restrictions placed on him by others of his profession and the Medical Society?

"Did he perhaps mention a specific case that he was particularly concerned about or had assisted with?" I then asked.

"Anything at all that might provide a clue to what he was working on? Perhaps a recent patient with a difficult injury, a new treatment that might not have been looked favorably upon by others at St. James?"

"There was a case some months ago," she hesitated.

"Please continue."

"A young boy. Joseph is so partial to children. We cannot have children, but he has always been particularly taken with them and anything he might do to help them. The boy was injured quite severely when he was attacked by one of his father's hunting hounds. It was an accident to be certain, the child was teasing the animal and it had lunged at him.

"According to my husband, the boy's face was badly injured, however, it seems that he was able to repair most of the damage."

I wondered what the boy's parents might be able to tell me about the injury and the child's recovery.

"I understand that Dr. Bennett has published a book about some of his cases and his work. Publishing can be such a daunting process. Might I see it?" I inquired.

She looked at me with some surprise and for the first time I caught a faint smile.

"Of course, although I don't know what you hope to find. I tried to read it once and gave up— all the medical terms and that sort of thing that meant nothing to me. I'll get it for you."

She rose and briefly left the parlor. She returned a short time later.

The book was impressive in size with embossed leather binding.

"Might I take it with me?"

There was a look of surprise.

"I suppose there is no harm... if it will help in any way."

She was obviously doubtful in that regard.

"Of course you may take it. I understand that you are published as well."

I didn't go into that, as my efforts were somewhat different than a medical procedural text. I then inquired about the name of the little boy's family.

"I have no idea how that might be useful, but of course." She wrote down the name of the family and handed it to me.

"Do you believe that some accident may have befallen my husband?"

I knew from Brodie that it was often better not to mention possible theories that often only had the effect of causing more distress for families.

"I have some additional inquiries that I want to make," I replied and thanked her for meeting with me, along with the name of the young patient and his family as well as the doctor's book.

What more might I learn?

The hound had disappeared during the time that I met with Mrs. Bennett. He returned abruptly as I left the building at Belgrave Square with something suspicious in his mouth.

I absolutely did not want to examine it any closer to determine what it might be.

"Drop that! Or you are not coming with me." I ordered, with absolutely no idea how much he understood, or cared to for that matter.

However, he did drop the object which I did hope was not some possession of someone at Belgrave Square, or something more personal such as a hand or foot which I thought unlikely at a second glance.

He sat upon the walk as I waited for the cab that Mrs. Bennett had called for me. I ignored more than one curious glance of those who passed by. I had to admit that the hound was hardly the small, fluffy sort that might be carried along in my arms or my bag.

"Is everything all right, miss?" asked a woman who looked to be someone's housekeeper by the bag she carried with wrapped packages that might have been from the grocer.

"Yes, quite." I replied. "He's a companion of my... husband's and occasionally follows along." I thanked her as I contemplated that word that had popped in. Husband.

Hmmm. And that of course, led to the next thought—wife!

Of the different titles I'd had, that seemed the strangest, quite simply because I had never considered it before.

I was niece to my great-aunt. I was sister to Linnie. At one time I had been my parents' daughter. I was an author. I had been described as an adventuress, whatever that was supposed to mean.

And then there was the title I had inherited from our father, *Lady* Forsythe, which I found to be cumbersome and somewhat off-putting, but there it was. And now... wife! How very strange!

The driver arrived and I climbed inside, the hound leaping in after. He was getting quite good at that, and without the usual warning snarl at the driver which had a way of putting some ill at ease.

I gave the driver the address of the office on the Strand. There was information I wanted to add to the chalkboard.

Sir William Pettigrew was the father of the young boy who had been injured and had then sought the services of Dr. Bennett. I would send round a message and inquire if it was possible to meet.

I also wanted to meet with Munro regarding inquiries he was making among those he knew, and that would give me the opportunity to see how Lily was doing with her lessons, particularly after that somewhat unusual piano recital.

I have learned not to be surprised where my great-aunt is concerned. She had lived long enough that she had seen or experienced most things a woman might in life.

A member of the ton, she had been born to her title of Duchess, however she rarely used it. According to family archives she was a direct descendant of King William— William the Conqueror that is, almost a thousand years earlier.

There was a rather antiquated sword in the sword room that had been documented to have been used by the Conqueror. And in consideration of that man's exploits, some rather colorful to be certain according to history, it did perhaps explain certain traits.

My aunt had never encountered a man, high-born or low for that matter, whom she couldn't persuade to her way of thinking. I had been told recently that I seemed to have inherited that particular quality.

I had spoken with my sister earlier. She had shared a familiar comment.

*"You really must do something with her..."*

The call had ended abruptly and I could only imagine who she was referring to. In the past, it had been my aunt, referring to her plans to go on safari in Africa which had been set aside due to an ankle injury.

I had my suspicions about that as my sister was in residence at the time following her divorce. However, I would not want to think that she might have gone to such extremes to waylay our aunt from her plans... which had only been temporarily delayed.

Then there was Lily. It was very possible that Linnie was referring to her and some peccadillo she had committed.

I did brace myself for what I might encounter as my coach pulled through the gates of Sussex Square.

I was met at the door by my aunt's head butler.

"Good day, Mr. Symons."

"Lady Forsythe," he acknowledged. "Or should I say Madame Brodie?"

*Madame?*

I shuddered at that. It did sound quite ancient. And as for the other part of it? I was still adjusting to that.

"Mr. Symons, you have known me since I was in nappies, and then after Miss Lenore and I came to live here. You have certainly witnessed some of my more colorful adventures as well as a few of my transgressions."

"Quite so," he replied in that very proper way of a head butler.

"Including that rather unforgivable incident when I appropriated the pot of glue from the coach barn and glued your trousers to the kitchen chair when you sat for evening meal," I reminded him.

"A memorable encounter, miss."

"An encounter that required your trousers to be cut away from the chair, and then a new pair of trousers." I recalled.

"Which her ladyship was most considerate of, and most generous," he replied. "Although she did suggest that I inspect any chair before sitting in it from that day forward, miss."

"Exactly," I told him. "Therefore in recognition of my past transgressions, you should continue to call me Miss Mikaela, and not Madame. It reminds me of Madame Lucretia Vandervere." I leaned in close.

"Between you and me, a dreadful woman." I could have sworn there was a sudden quirk of a smile, that was quickly gone, considering his position.

"I quite understand, miss. You will find the ladies in the small salon. I believe her ladyship called it a spa treatment, although I have no idea what that might mean. I do believe that it includes vegetables."

Spa treatment? Oh, dear.

Along with my sister's comment in that earlier telephone conversation, I nodded and proceeded toward the small salon that adjoined the garden room that had been transformed into the replica of a jungle during my aunt's safari planning.

I was grateful that the monkey had found its way back to the zoo after being on loan to my aunt. However, it most certainly would have provided entertainment for Lily. Not that my aunt's household had ever been lacking in that regard.

There was always something exciting or at least interesting. I suppose it accounted for our childhood that had been regarded somewhat unusual.

It wasn't everyone who had the adventures of running loose about the highlands of Scotland or exploring ancient places. According to one of my great-aunt's friends, it undoubtedly accounted for my wild and unpredictable nature, whatever that might mean. But there you are.

In retrospect, I was grateful that my adventures hadn't been limited to museums and art galleries and wouldn't have changed a thing.

I now stopped at the entrance to the small salon and stared at the scene before me. My aunt lay across one of the settees, my sister upon the other, while Lily lay on the carpet on the floor.

Anyone else coming upon this scenario might be inclined to panic, or a shout-out to the household staff to summon the family physician. Anyone else, that is.

Behind me, Mr. Symons announced my arrival with a not-subtle clearing of the throat.

"Miss Mikaela," he announced, which immediately brought Lily upright, followed by my sister.

"Oh, miss!" Lily exclaimed as she scrambled to her feet. Then in true Lily fashion exclaimed, "I've lost the damned vegetables again!"

"A lady does not curse," my aunt reminded her. It was admirable on her part, however her efforts had fallen short with myself at that age.

The loss of the "damned vegetables" sent Lily scrambling to retrieve said vegetables that had scattered across the carpet—slices of cucumber by the look of it.

I assisted, having previously been through this particular ritual of my aunt's, who was still reclined with slices of said vegetable in place upon her eyes.

"Is that you, Mikaela dear?" my aunt called out.

"Yes, I'm here to see Mr. Munro," I replied. "If he's about."

And without moving a muscle. "He returned some time ago... then out and about again on some matter or another again," she replied without dislodging a single cucumber slice.

Was that some matter or another the inquiries I had asked him to make regarding Dr. Bennett?

Lily leaned in close. "Her ladyship says as how the vegetable is good for the skin and eyes," she explained. "I ain't never heard of that before," she exclaimed as we gathered scattered slices of cucumber.

"Anything like this always went into the cook pot at the Church. Mrs. Erditch, wot cooked for the ladies, was real particular about that. Nothin' was wasted."

And most certainly not for placing slices of cucumber over the eyes and cheeks, I thought.

"I heard Mr. Munro tell her ladyship that he wouldna be back for evenin' supper, he had someone he needed to see," Lily added. "Seemed right important."

I did hope that he might have learned something important regarding Dr. Bennett's disappearance.

"Mikaela, dear," my aunt called out, once more with every slice of "damned" vegetable securely in place.

"I am hosting a bit of a soiree tomorrow evening in celebration of Sir James' return to London. I do hope that you will be able to attend, and Mr. Brodie of course. You and Sir James shared those earlier adventures and he must have new ones?"

Though the invitation was more or less in the form of a question, there was actually no question involved. When my aunt extended an invitation it was assumed that it would be accepted.

Not that she commanded attendance. However...

"Of course," I replied.

"Eight o'clock, dear," she added, then went back to her cucumbers.

After retrieving several slices, Lily and I removed to the library with the excuse of learning more about her progress with her lessons. As soon as the door closed I retrieved a deck of cards from the drawer in the game table.

"Lessons, indeed!" Linnie commented as she found us in a heated game of poker and announced supper.

I tallied up the sum I had lost to Lily and promised to pay her when I returned to Mayfair as I rarely carried anything larger than cab fare. The girl had an incredible talent for the game.

We had just finished supper and dessert was to be served in the formal salon when Mr. Aldrich, my aunt's footman, announced that Munro had returned and requested to meet with me.

I excused myself and met with him in the office off the kitchen.

"You've learned something?"

"Aye," he replied.

He had removed the black wool jacket that now hung on a hook on the wall across from the desk. At a glance it was damp from the weather.

"This afternoon, I spoke to a man who provided the name of someone who made unusual deliveries to a tenement in Aldgate, just across from the ironworks. After a good sum and several pints, he provided the name of the man, a fellow by the name of Darby."

"What was unusual about the deliveries?"

"In the first place, that part of Aldgate isna the sort of place where others make deliveries. Those who live in that part of London are poor and the best they can afford are the scraps left from market and handouts. As for the rents..."

"I see your point. What about the items that were delivered?"

"According to what the man I spoke with heard, the deliveries weren't food or cast offs that might be the usual for those in that part of the city. They were instruments and some sort of medical supplies."

I might not have thought anything of it, except for that last part; medical supplies. While it seemed a remote possibility that a location in Aldgate had anything to do with Dr. Bennett, still...

"When was this?"

"The first delivery was three months ago, then several more after. It was a lucrative connection for the driver."

"Have you been able to make contact with the driver? A name of the person to whom the deliveries were made?" I then asked.

"No. The driver worked independent as opposed to one of the usual companies one can hire about the city for such things."

His expression indicated there was more.

"He died in a stramash outside a tavern some six weeks ago, stabbed through the heart."

A coincidence?

Another crime among many across the city, and particularly in the East End where there was so much poverty and few enough of the Metropolitan Police. And then, as I had learned, there were those who simply looked the other way. As I had also learned from Brodie, there was no such thing as a coincidence.

"Do you know where the tenement is in Aldgate?"

"I can find it well enough by the description from the man I spoke with. It's across from a leather shop. I came back for this."

He opened the drawer of the desk and retrieved a revolver, very much the same as Brodie carried.

"I'm going with you," I announced. "I can be ready immediately."

"No."

I had heard before, and suspected that it was something most particular to Scots, a simple word that was more like a command.

"Brodie would not approve."

"I most certainly will go with you or on my own, if need be. I'm certain that I can find the tenement you described. Or someone on the street who can assist."

How difficult could it possibly be? A tenement across from a leather shop in Aldgate.

Munro swore under his breath, quite colorfully actually. But then I had heard that before as well.

And where the devil *was* Brodie?

Brodie met with Herr Schmidt at the German Gymnasium.

They knew one another from a previous inquiry case, introduced by Mikaela Forsythe.

It was a surprise in the least to discover that the woman who was a client at the time had some expertise in certain sporting disciplines as it was called. More particularly in the use of a sword— a rapier she had called it —and had then proceeded to provide a demonstration.

He needed the man's assistance in the matter of rumors that the anarchist, Soropkin, might be in the country or more precisely in London, according to different reports Alex Sinclair had deciphered.

Schmidt was German and the men and women who frequented the gymnasium encountered those from different immigrant communities about the East End.

It was like a pot where every sort was thrown together no matter how much they attempted to keep to themselves— a name overheard; a rumor passed along at the open stalls on the street. A man like Soropkin wouldn't go unnoticed no matter how much he kept to the shadows.

It was possible that someone knew something, and that it would eventually find its way to Herr Schmidt.

Brodie had dressed in rough cambric trousers, a turtleneck sweater, and long wool coat of the sort the seamen wore, all in black, along with a worn black cap that he wore when he wanted to move about unseen or at least where no one would give him a second glance.

"Don't use my name," Schmidt had told him. "It would be bad for business for others to know that I was helping one of the Met."

He had reminded Schmidt that he was no longer with the Metropolitan Police, but in private inquiries now.

"And Fraulein Forsythe?" Schmidt had inquired. "She is well?"

Brodie assured him that she was. He had been in contact with Munro. He knew that she had been making inquiries on behalf of the case she had been working on. That should keep her occupied until he could obtain enough information to hand this particular matter over to Sir Avery.

"She is well," he assured Schmidt. "Currently on other business."

He didn't explain further. There was no purpose in it, so long as the man would assist in the matter.

Schmidt had nodded. "If I was not already married to my Anna," he had looked across his desk, his meaning unmistakable.

"Then again, with Miss Forsythe's skills, and her spirit..." He shook his head. "I think it would not be wise. But it would be most exciting. No?" he asked with a hearty laugh in that way of men.

Most definitely, Brodie thought at the time. He knew that well enough.

Schmidt had given him a name— Heilman, another German, who worked at the Thames Ironworks and Shipbuilders at the Victoria Docks. He was a sort of self-appointed mayor over the German community. People heard things and passed them along to him in a place where their safety might be in keeping watch over others.

"Tell him I sent ya and that it's in the matter of Soropkin. He'll help ya if he knows anything. The anarchist is a bad sort. There's many of us who have had experience with the man or know those who have and would as soon be rid of him."

Along with the information he had from Alex regarding the man, the sooner he was able to determine what Soropkin was doing in London, the better.

After his meeting with Schmidt, he set off for the iron-works. The day shift was about to end, and he wanted to speak with Heilman and find out what he knew.

He caught the tram out to the Victoria Docks at Bow Creek on the Thames.

The ironworks was a sprawling beast of a place on the east bank, a railway to the Thames wharf on another with direct access to the river for ships under construction.

It was very near the end of the twelve-hour shift when he arrived and caught a trolley to the main gate where workers arrived and departed. From there he was directed to the super-visor's office where he was told that Heilman might be found as he had not yet left for the day.

Brodie was accustomed to the reserve, even outright hostil-ity, of those among the immigrant communities against outsiders from his work for the Met. It was no different with Heilman, who at first appeared to speak very little English, a common response.

"I'm looking for a man by the name of Soropkin. Or he might go by another name." Brodie gave him the only descrip-tion that Sir Avery had, taken from a photograph that was several years old.

"Herr Schmidt said that you might be able to provide information about him."

There was that long stare as Brodie stood in the doorway of the small office that was no more than a storeroom with a desk and a chair, and were covered with the grime and iron tailings, fine as powder, that sifted through from the bank of furnaces in the massive building.

"Soropkin?" Heilman repeated as if he had only just heard the name. He continued to stare at Brodie. Then as if he had decided something, he gave a jerk of his head toward the door. Brodie closed it.

"Soropkin," Heilman repeated. *"Der hurensohn,"* he spat out. "What you English call a son of a bitch; a cold-blooded murderer— men, women, children, it doesn't matter in the name of his cause." Then, "Sit down, Mr. Brodie, and tell me what *you* know about Soropkin and the reason you are looking for him."

It seemed that Heilman spoke very good English when he chose too.

Over the next hour, Brodie explained the information the Agency had come upon, that Soropkin *was* somewhere in London.

The fact that he was there was not something to be ignored. If he had something planned against the British government, then he had to be stopped.

"You are not English by birth," Heilman pointed out.

"No," Brodie replied, a situation that many Scots refused to accept— the English authority over Scotland, a centuries old battle that some insisted was not ended, merely waiting to rekindle.

And yet here he was, on behalf of protecting the very

crown that had held Scotland under the boot for centuries. But Soropkin was another matter, and it was here and now.

"What can ye tell me about him?" Brodie brought the conversation back round to the reason he was there.

"What have ye heard through yer people?"

"Why should I help you?" Heilman demanded.

"If he succeeds in some plan, then this," Brodie made a gesture to the vast cavern of the ironworks beyond the office, "may be burnt to the ground like most of the city along with the jobs of those men, and yerself. If ye survive.

"Ye claim to know of the man's brutality, the deaths he has caused. I ask for yer help. If ye refuse to give it, ye are no better than the man ye hate so well and will have the blood of those who die because of it on yer hands. Yer own family perhaps as well when ye came here for the chance at a better life."

"What do you know of a better life?"

"I know about fighting to survive on the streets, and to my way of thinking, wot I have now is worth fighting to hold onto."

For several moments, Heilman merely looked at him. Then he slowly nodded. "I will tell you what I have heard."

What he knew was only rumor, but he trusted where those the rumors came from. Soropkin was in London. But no one had actually seen him.

It was safe to assume that he was there for one purpose as Brodie and Sir Avery feared, to instigate a situation that Europe had seen in no less than a half dozen cities over the past two years.

It might be demonstrations in the streets, attacks on certain people in positions of power, or possibly as in Munich months earlier— a bomb set off at a prominent place or event.

It was impossible to know, but the rumors had people in

the German community uneasy, watchful, yet as he said, the man hadn't actually been seen by anyone on the streets. He was like a ghost, there one minute, gone the next.

The last word Heilman had about Soropkin was that he was rumored to have been seen in another part of London. But it made no sense. It was far from anything that might have been the sort of target the anarchist preferred— areas of power and influence.

"You will find him?" Heilman asked as Brodie thanked him and stood to leave.

He nodded, then left. He had the name of the man who heard where Soropkin was last seen.

Munro cursed for what must have been the dozenth time since leaving Sussex Square as the driver of the cab we had taken across London collected his fare then snapped the reins and disappeared down the street.

We had returned first to the office on the Strand after Munro insisted on placing a telephone call to Brodie. There had been no answer, nor had he been there according to Mr. Cavendish.

Munro left word for Brodie, then reluctantly agreed that I could accompany him after the threat I had made earlier.

We set off on foot in the direction he had described for the tenement in Aldgate, just across from a leather shop. The driver had been most accommodating in finding it. Imagine that.

"Damned stubborn woman," Munro muttered.

I had been called that in the past and considered it a compliment.

"Ye'll do exactly as I say," he added.

Of course.

I had seen such buildings before in the inquiry cases Brodie and I took on, in other parts of London and Edinburgh as well. It was always disconcerting to see the poverty, the cramped conditions, sometimes two or three families to a flat; rats that ran the streets searching for garbage, a beggar who loomed up out of the shadows, only to disappear again as Munro warned him to leave off.

I couldn't help but think of Lily and what might have awaited her in a handful of years, spirited as she was. Here, I saw firsthand what destroyed one's spirit; the lights of the tavern where a young woman might be purchased for the night for the cost of a pint of ale, with no opportunity to survive much less change one's life.

Munro snapped at me, no translation needed, and I hurried to keep up with him.

"Ye have the revolver Brodie gave ye?" he asked as we crossed the street at the leather shop.

I assured him that I had, my fingers brushing the cold steel barrel of the weapon in the pocket of my skirt.

"There doesna seem to be anyone around," he nodded toward the two-story building. "Could be the tenants were turned out."

I knew it was a possibility. With the winter there were fewer jobs. Fewer jobs meant less pay, or none at all. If there was no pay a family might persuade the landlord to extend them a month, but no more. Then they were out on the street.

This was the world where Munro and Brodie had lived, and by the darkened windows over the first floor it seemed that might be the situation.

There were many abandoned buildings in London crumbling into disrepair. Some were claimed by the city as it expanded roadways and thoroughfares.

Others, some built more than two centuries earlier, were either torn down or left to the rats and people on the street who might sleep there for a night or two before being turned out by the neighborhood watch.

Some stayed longer and built fires to keep warm. The fire brigade was kept busy with buildings thought to be abandoned that turned into an inferno. In most places like this there was nothing to be done but to let it burn, and try to prevent it from spreading to other buildings.

"Ye're to stay behind me," Munro told her as they approached the main entrance of the tenement.

It hardly seemed possible as he shone a handheld light at the front doors. They had been chained shut with a sign posted — *Do not enter by order of the London Magistrate.*

Munro's source of information had been certain this was the location. I laid a hand on his arm and gestured to the sagging railing along the walkway that led to a lower level. We followed the railing to the steps that descended to a doorway below.

The door was slightly ajar. He pushed me back to what he undoubtedly considered a safer distance, then turned toward the door, revolver in hand.

It would have been wise to simply wait for him to make a cursory inspection. However...

I followed him into the lower level below the tenement that the Magistrate's people had obviously failed to secure. Or possibly not if one went by the splintered frame of the door. Munro slowly swept the handheld light across the walls, floor, and door that obviously led deeper into the below street level basement of the building.

Munro moved on ahead, his light playing across the door. He slowly pushed it open.

A putrid smell swept toward me and choked my throat, bringing back a vivid memory from my travel years before on the Nile when a man's body was trapped in the water against the dock while the flies swarmed.

The smell was the same, of rotting flesh. Munro shouted and the handheld torch flew out of his hand, hit the floor and then went out. I had no idea where he was as I was thrown back against the door.

The air momentarily knocked out of me, I did the only thing that came to mind and reacted instinctively. I pulled back my fist and sent a blow as hard as I could in the direction of whoever had shoved me.

With only the light from those stained windows at the street level, it was admittedly not my best move, but it was enough to bring a startled curse.

I took advantage of our assailant's surprise and swept his feet from under him. He hit the floor with a groan and another curse as I thrust my hand into my bag and retrieved the revolver.

"Mikaela?!"

That stopped me as I pulled back the hammer and prepared to defend myself and Munro if necessary.

"What the bloody devil are ye doin' here?!" the "assailant" on the floor demanded in that broad Scots accent that I knew quite well.

"I think ye broke my nose!"

# Eight

I STOOD across the office from Brodie.

"So good to see you again," I commented as I laid the revolver he had given me on the desk.

There was not an immediate comment as he pressed a cold cloth across his nose which seemed to have quit bleeding, with a rather colorful bruise below his left eye.

Both eyes, one quite narrowed, glaring back at me.

"What the bloody devil were ye doin' there, woman?!"

That did seem to be the question of the hour, or perhaps as much as he could demand that wasn't a litany of curses, some of which I had not heard before.

Imagine that.

I removed my jacket and crossed over to the coat rack.

"I might ask the same of you."

Perhaps not the right response under the circumstances, said circumstances that had Munro leaving immediately after we reached the office, obviously with experience in such matters in consideration of their long friendship. Those "*mat-*

*ters"* such as the one I now confronted in the form of a very angry Scot.

"Your inquiries for Sir Avery?" I ventured a guess.

"And yerself?" he demanded.

"My inquiries on behalf of Helen Bennett," I informed him.

I had indeed discovered where Dr. Bennett had been keeping himself the past several days. The question now was what had happened and what was he doing in that part of London in what appeared to be a well-equipped medical office. Or perhaps *"clinic"* was a better description by what we found there.

It was apparent that Dr. Joseph Bennett had set up practice in that abandoned tenement building. But for what reason when he very obviously had an office and medical practice at St. James Hospital?

Dr. Pennington had called him brilliant, even though he had been criticized and apparently censured for some of the methods he promoted which, according to Helen Bennett, had the potential to greatly improve the lives of severely injured patients.

Was he then forced to set up a secret practice in Aldgate because of that censure, a brilliant physician forced to take other measures to continue his practice? Or for some other reason?

"Did it occur to ye that it could be dangerous?"

The anger behind that question brought me back to Brodie. He was quite irritated over the matter as he pulled off his blood-stained sweater— that blow I landed had caused his nose to bleed quite profusely.

If it had been anyone else but Brodie, I would have felt a sense of satisfaction. However...

I was not entirely unsympathetic, which of course raised the question of what precisely was he doing at that tenement in Aldgate?

He tossed his sweater through the doorway into the adjacent room, and I was forced to view Brodie in rough cambric pants and boots, overlong hair somewhat disheveled with several days of dark beard, and that cloth clutched to one side of his face.

I was reminded that Brodie could be quite a stirring sight. Not given to slack muscles or paunchiness as a good many men were inclined, but quite lean and well-muscled, with that light dusting of dark hair on his chest.

It had been some days since we had last been together at the office I thought, as I took inventory. Although that glare from those dark eyes was a bit off-putting.

"The answer is yes and I took all precautions, the exact reason Munro accompanied me since you have been unavailable the past few weeks," I pointed out.

"And the reason *you* were there?" I continued. "I'm not interested in any excuse about some 'highly sensitive inquiries' that Sir Avery has sent you on."

"Highly sensitive, and dangerous inquiries," he replied.

I gave him a long look. He was deliberately trying to antagonize me. Two could play at this game.

"And it would seem that our separate inquiries have crossed paths." I pointed out the obvious and retrieved a bottle of Old Lodge whisky from the drawer in the file cabinet.

He did look as if he could use a bit of my aunt's whisky. I poured two glasses, handed him one, then crossed the office and proceeded to set coal in the firebox as icy rain pelted the window.

"It appears that we might be able to assist one another," I

stated the obvious as I dusted off my hands, and stood once more to face a thoroughly disgruntled Scot.

"By God, Mikaela!" He held out his glass for another dram. "What if there had been someone else there instead of meself?"

"Munro has proven himself more than capable of handling such situations."

"Ye shouldn't have been there at all!" he roared at me.

I poured us both another dram.

"Nevertheless..." I handed his glass to him.

The sound of the bell on the landing cut off a string of curses.

I went to the door and found a bucket tied to the rope that had been used in the past to send packages, particularly food, aloft by Mr. Cavendish.

I glanced over the railing to the alcove below. He was in his usual place, caught sight of me, and nodded.

There had been a brief conversation when Mr. Cavendish took one look at Brodie as we were turned from Aldgate.

"An encounter in a pub, was it? Ye'll need ice for that." He had then set off on his rolling platform in the direction of the Public House across the Strand.

That had sent Brodie off on another tirade that included another string of curses that continued to the present.

I unhooked the bucket that contained a good amount of ice in it and returned to the office.

I walked over, seized the folded cloth Brodie had pressed over his eye, and proceeded to wrap ice in it. I handed it back to him.

"Ye seem to have some knowledge of such things," he commented, somewhat more civil as he held the ice pack against his face.

It was one of those little things I'd learned in my early

childhood from assisting my father when he returned after a night at his club. This was different, the man was different, but the remedy the same.

"I've had some practice," I replied.

Before I could step away, his other hand closed over my wrist.

"If something had happened and I wasna there..."

"You were there," I pointed out. "And Munro as well."

"Ye're my wife!" he roared at me. "Aldgate is no place for ye... And an abandoned tenement where a man has been murdered?"

"The man was the husband of our client and I was following up on information I had in the matter," I explained with the distinct impression that he was not listening.

There was definitely something more that had him stirred up. While I appreciated the fact that he was concerned about me, still he knew that I was quite capable of taking care of myself. He had, after all, given me the revolver and I had proven myself to be more than competent.

"Damn woman!" he swore and then tossed aside the cold wrap and came at me.

"Ye try a man's soul, Mikaela Forsythe! I should be well rid of ye, but God help us both...!"

I have perfected a fairly accurate ability to assess a person's demeanor, in particular, Brodie's. However, considering his anger, misplaced as I considered it to be at the moment, he caught me quite unaware.

He kissed me!

Not the sort of kiss one might have expected after not seeing one another for almost two weeks, but one that was far different.

This was Brodie. Bloody stubborn Scot! Unpredictable,

forceful, not one I could easily maneuver my way around. He could be so very aggravating.

However there was that scent of orange and cinnamon about him that I had missed most dreadfully...

"Why would a man as educated and accomplished as Dr. Bennett set up an office in the basement of that tenement in Aldgate?" I asked the question that had been lurking at the back of my thoughts since the previous evening as I stood before the chalkboard where I had made my notes.

"That is the question."

I waited for Brodie's usual response when we approached an inquiry case together.

I had shared what I knew about the Bennett case, but he had shared little beyond the fact that I knew he was making inquiries for the Agency.

Instead of a comment or imparting some information about that, there was a curse from the adjoining room.

Brodie appeared in a fresh shirt, a tie hanging loose about his neck, wool trousers and boots, dressed this morning some-what more refined than his *stalking attire* as I called it.

He had obviously attempted to tie the tie and now glared at me from one eye, the other one somewhat bruised and quite colorful from the blow I'd landed the previous evening.

I pushed his hands aside and proceeded to tie the typical four-in-hand style that he preferred when forced to wear one.

It did give him a somewhat dashing appearance, which I had commented on previously. I suspected it had something to do with the contrast of the refined clothes of a gentleman with his overlong dark hair and beard.

At the time, he had made a typically Scottish sound that described precisely what he thought of that.

However, a clean shirt and tie could mean only one thing. He was to meet with Sir Avery at the Tower, something I was quite determined to be part of particularly after the events of the previous evening as I seized both ends of the tie and refused to be intimidated by that dark glare.

"Where did ye learn such a thing as to tie the damned things?"

I suspected there was more behind the question, possibly an unasked question about the man in particular who taught me?

I let him think on that for a moment more before replying.

"Mr. Symons, my aunt's head butler."

He had taught me as a child when I had made quite a nuisance of myself over the matter. He had indulged me in the fascinating art of tying a man's tie.

"As odd as that sounds, it makes perfect sense considerin' yer ways."

I smiled as I felt that dark gaze on me. I crossed the two ends of the gray silk tie one over the other, then once more around, created the loop, tucked the one through, then smoothed the wide knot I had created.

"Ye have gentle hands," Brodie commented, apparently somewhat mollified. "I noticed that about ye from the verra beginning."

Ah, possibly at our first, quite memorable encounter?

Of all the things he had said about me over almost two years, and then when in Scotland during that most unexpected proposal, this was something quite different.

He laid his hand over mine, much as he had the night before when the anger had spent itself and we had finally retired for the night to that adjacent room. His hand had covered mine very much the same way then, those long strong fingers wrapping around mine as I lay against him.

"*She* had gentle hands that could ease a hurt or the anger. Ye're like that— most of the time," he added.

I knew that he spoke of his mother, whom he had lost all those years before, the brutality of it leaving him to the streets of Edinburgh and then London.

Not that I had replaced her or even that he thought of it that way. But it was a loss that he carried, perhaps always would, the senselessness of it, someone he had cared deeply for who had cared for him. Then gone.

I understood as perhaps only someone who had experienced similar losses, and fiercely protected those who mattered to me — my sister, our great-aunt, and quite unexpectedly the man who stood before me. There was someone else now as well. Lily.

I touched his cheek with that understanding, my fingers brushing his beard.

"I'll not lose ye, lass," he told me then. "I couldna bear it."

I realized then the true reason he hadn't wanted me to be part of the inquiries he was making for Sir Avery.

However, here we were and we both knew that I wasn't going to simply accept waiting at home like the obedient wife. That was not part of the *"arrangement."*

"I suppose you will simply have to accept the fact that you will have to include me when you go off on your inquiries for Sir Avery," I replied, then added, "to keep me safe."

I did understand that somewhat archaic way he had of looking at things.

"However, you must admit that I have proven myself to be most capable in such situations."

He made one of those typically Scottish sounds, more a groan I thought. But didn't argue the point. And I smiled to myself.

There were moments when I managed to outmaneuver him. Not that I objected to those occasional outbursts of male anger.

After the dust cleared as they say, was most pleasant.

I accompanied Brodie to the Agency offices in the Tower of London. Our two inquiry cases had crossed paths after the discovery of Dr. Bennett's somewhat bloated and decaying body in that tenement basement in Aldgate. It appeared that one obviously connected to the other.

"The question," Sir Avery concluded after we had both provided what we each knew in the matter, "would seem to be, how is it connected. Miss Forsythe, you seem to have resolved the matter of Dr. Bennett's disappearance, but it does not explain the reason for the location that would indicate the need for secrecy."

"I believe it may have to do with the fact that some aspects of Dr. Bennett's work were censured by the Society of Medicine," I provided. "It was a known fact that he was quite resentful of it."

Sir Avery nodded, one hand against his chin, his expression grim.

"Your thoughts, Mr. Brodie?" he then asked.

"I agree as far we know. The next question would be the reason for the murder. There were items of value in the rooms that could easily be sold to the right people on the street, yet they were still there. There is no way of knowing if money might have been stolen in the process."

"Robbery was then not the motive," Sir Avery concluded.

"So it would seem."

"And what of the manner of the physician's death?" Sir Avery asked.

I listened with interest as Brodie replied with an expertise that came from experience.

"With a blade to the throat. The artery at the neck was severed by a precise cut."

"You are not a surgeon, Mr. Brodie."

"One doesn't need to be a surgeon to recognize such a wound. It was meant for one purpose and one only, and it accomplished that in a matter of a seconds, no more."

"And in the matter of Soropkin?" Sir Avery then asked.

"He was supposedly seen in Aldgate and had made inquiries on the street regarding the tenement."

"Is the source of that information reliable?"

"As reliable as a good amount of the drink and a crown note would purchase."

"Then the answer is, perhaps, perhaps not."

I was aware that Brodie had a certain hesitation where Sir Avery was concerned. It had been glaringly obvious during the matter of our previous inquiries in Scotland in the matter of his mother's murder some years before. Most particularly in the matter of a "reliable source" of information.

It was apparent that Brodie remembered that incident quite well.

"It is as reliable as the information acquired by Sholto McQueen."

That brought Sir Avery's head up.

"An unfortunate situation. Mr. McQueen had proven to be a reliable source in the past."

The man ended up dead in an attempt to play both ends against the middle as the saying went— providing information to Sir Avery and thereby to Brodie at the same time he was taking payments from someone on the other side of the "unfortunate situation."

I shifted in my chair, quite ready for the meeting to be at an end. I caught a look from Brodie, that subtle narrowing of that bruised gaze, and an almost imperceptible shake of the head.

"Precisely," Brodie then replied. Sir Avery looked up sharply.

"You will need to pursue your inquiries for the reasons we have already discussed. That coded message we intercepted came at a high price, a man's life.

"Time is of the essence, particularly if we accept that your source's sighting of Soropkin is correct. There is obviously more to this. And what the devil happened to you?" This was directed at Brodie.

"A brief encounter on the street," he replied.

Avery looked at me then, dismissively. Not something I accepted well.

"It would appear, Miss Forsythe, that your inquiries on behalf of the doctor's wife, are concluded. I will see that Dr. Bennett's body is retrieved and his wife appropriately notified."

I caught the warning look from Brodie. He did know me particularly well. However, warning, or no...

"Mrs. Bennett is *our* client and deserving of our care. *I* will call upon her and tell her of her husband's death. I'm certain you understand," I informed him in my best imitation of my great-aunt when dealing with someone who had the misfortune to challenge her on some matter. She had been a source of great inspiration for most of my life.

With that I turned and left Sir Avery's office and went in search of Alex Sinclair. I had questions about something Sir Avery had mentioned about that message that had been intercepted.

"Ye were a bit abrupt with Sir Avery," Brodie commented when he found me in Alex's office, discussing the reasons he couldn't possibly show me that message.

"Although, he deserved it, and ye do have a way with words."

I caught the undertone of approval.

"I thought it was perhaps better than dumping him to the floor. He's a good deal like the Chief Inspector."

Chief Inspector Abberline that is, with whom I had found myself at cross-purposes in the past. Not something I was going to forget or forgive, as it had been most serious.

"Noticed that, have ya?"

I heard the smile behind the words. I had missed that as well the last couple of weeks. We were both ignoring Alex. He cleared his throat to draw our attention.

Alex Sinclair was a most engaging young man with a shock of dark brown hair that was constantly falling across his forehead when he was excited about something. Most usually my young friend Lucy Penworth who also worked at the Agency.

"I haven't been able to decipher this yet and it cut off at the end. I did try to re-establish communication, but without success."

Brodie studied the message, a mix of letters and numbers.

"Sir Avery said to keep at it. But it's not something I've seen before."

"Nor would you be expected to," Brodie told him.

"Can you make a copy of this?" I inquired. Brodie looked at me with more than a little surprise.

"Now ye're a cryptologist?"

"No, however I am well read and I've seen a good many symbols and foreign letters in my travels. Perhaps there is something familiar in the message that might be helpful," I reasoned.

"That is not for other eyes," he reminded me.

"I perfectly understand. However, if you trust me, and, I am also well trusted by Prince Edward," I added from a previous case that involved my friend Templeton who was rumored to have had an affair with him.

"Surely I can be trusted now."

Brodie nodded at Alex. "I'll take responsibility, and it will give me the opportunity to examine it as well. And mind ye, ye're to let me know if ye figure out wot the bloody thing says."

Alex nodded. "I'll make you a copy, Miss Forsythe. It's not a long message and will only take a few minutes. I would appreciate it if you would not mention this to Sir Avery."

"I could always say that I struck you over the head and stole it from you while you were rendered unconscious," I suggested.

Alex gave Brodie a long look, most particularly at the bruise quite colorful about his left eye.

"That... won't be necessary, Miss Forsythe."

I placed a telephone call to Helen Bennett before leaving the Tower and requested to meet with her.

"*You have some word?*" she asked.

I heard the hesitation in her voice as I explained that I would prefer to speak with her in person. There was something in her voice; something familiar from when my sister had gone missing and her maid found dead. The certainty that what I had to tell her was not what she had hoped for.

Brodie accompanied me.

"My aunt has planned some sort of reception for Sir James Redstone this evening," I told him as we found a driver and set off for Belgrave Square.

"The invitation is for both of us."

The long pause that followed was a familiar one. If it hadn't been an invitation from my great-aunt, he would have simply refused, preferring to have bones broken rather than attend what he referred to as a "society event."

And, I would much rather have had the time to read through Dr. Bennett's book, however...

There was no need to say the rest of it.

While I agreed with him and would much rather have spent the evening together at the office on the Strand or at the townhouse in consideration of the past weeks when we had been off on our individual inquiries, it very likely wasn't an invitation that we could refuse.

Helen Bennett met us at the door of the residence when we arrived rather than her housekeeper. The expression on her face was one I had seen before in our other inquiry cases.

No words were exchanged. She simply turned and led the way into the parlor. It was Brodie who confirmed what she already suspected in that calm way of his.

And then in that way that had somehow become our way in working together, I gently asked additional questions after what we had found the night before.

Was she aware that he had an office at another location? Had he ever spoken of any concern over a particular patient? Did he ever speak of other work he was doing?

I had observed from our first meeting that Helen Bennett was not the dithering sort given to hysterics or fainting. She was intelligent, calm, and had been forthcoming with any information that might assist no matter what the outcome might be.

She had respected her husband and had spoken proudly of his accomplishments. And now...?

We spoke of my meeting with Dr. Pennington, the fact that he considered Dr. Bennett to be quite brilliant, as well as certain aspects of her husband's work that were censured by the Society of Medicine.

"He was very hurt by that," she commented now. "Years of research... some of the procedures he found that were more than two thousand years old." She gathered herself.

"He felt that it was being set aside as unimportant." She looked at me then.

"You have a copy of his first book. It was written some years ago. After the reprimand from the president of the Society following lectures Joseph gave, he set about organizing his notes to publish a new book.

"The Society refused to endorse his work," she added. "As a result his publisher declined to publish the book."

I exchanged a look with Brodie. He knew what I was thinking.

"Do ye perhaps have his notes for that second book?" he asked.

She nodded. "They would be in the library where he often worked until late at night. Until recently..."

"They might be helpful if there was something he wrote about that might assist in our inquiry into his death," I suggested.

She provided us with the portfolio of Dr. Bennett's notes,

that included his research along with findings for that second book.

"You will tell me what you find."

I assured her that we would.

~

Now, I stared out the window of the coach as we left Belgrave Square.

What might I find? Anything that might tell us the reason he had that office in a poor part of London? A clue to the reason he was murdered?

Or perhaps nothing more than a man's obsession with techniques he wanted to bring to his profession that were frowned upon by others? Was that in itself a motive for murder?

I felt that dark gaze on me from across the coach.

"Ye are a rare woman, Mikaela."

Not the first time he had said that, and it wasn't that I didn't appreciate it. God knows I had been dismissed by a great many others with their opinions about my travels, my books, and now the inquiry cases we shared— an "amusing hobby" more than one had called it. Chief Inspector Abberline came to mind.

"Ye have a care for those we encounter. Not everyone understands."

Was he perhaps thinking of his own experiences? Or perhaps that first case that had been very personal to me.

"Life is cruel," I replied. "I cannot help but think of what will happen to her now."

"Helen Bennett strikes me as a strong person. Much like someone else I know."

Be that as it may. "I want to be able to give her answers for the reason he was murdered."

Brodie nodded. "And ye will. It's one of the things I admire about ye."

"Admire?" That seemed an odd word, considering his determination to keep me out of it, and the black eye I'd give him.

"Well, perhaps a bit more than that."

Perhaps. He *was* a man of few words, but I would take it.

With my aunt's soiree in mind and the day fast slipping away, we returned to Mayfair so that I could change my clothes.

I was not given to obsessing over a new gown to make an "appropriate appearance." I considered such things to be superficial and extremely annoying. I didn't have time for it, what with my usual schedule, my books, our inquiry cases, and...

However, Brodie reminded me that this was my aunt's soiree, and I should dress appropriately. I chose a gown that I had previously worn for some other occasion. When I stepped from my bedroom, Brodie frowned.

Did I sense an objection? "Hmmm," he made that sound that might have meant anything.

"It occurs to me that I might have to fend off admirers," he said then.

I did appreciate the compliment, as much of one as could be expected from a man who rarely commented on such things.

We then returned to the Strand so that he might change into something more "appropriate," with most of his clothes there since we had not as yet resolved the issue of where we were to live.

"Ye know what I think of these sorts of events. A soiree?"

"I assured him that he could always disappear with Munro into the cellar at Sussex Square until the festivities subsided.

"The cellar, ye say?" he replied with interest.

"There is, after all, a considerable amount of Old Lodge whisky stored there," I replied.

"Or... we could simply stay here, and send our regrets '*due to an unforeseen development in a case?*'" I suggested.

Those "unforeseen" developments could be most interesting. That dark gaze softened.

"And disappoint her ladyship?" he pointed out. "How might you explain that to her?"

He took my hand in his, those long fingers encircling mine as he turned my hand and kissed the palm. My fingers curled into the softness of his beard.

"She is not a woman without some experience," I replied.

"Aye, perhaps. But I would not want to be questioned about the reason we did not attend and be forced to tell her the truth."

He could be such a devil at times...

# Nine

SUSSEX SQUARE HAD BEEN TRANSFORMED.

My great-aunt is known for her soirees, as she calls them. Small, intimate, get-togethers from time-to-time, that just happen to rival those of royal celebrations.

It was always amazing to watch everything come together with the expertise of a general who commanded a vast army.

However, *"small and intimate"* may have been a slight exaggeration. The Duke of Wellington had nothing on Lady Antonia Montgomery when it came to organization, commanding a campaign, and then executing with precision.

"Bloody hell!" Brodie exclaimed, the lights of Sussex Square illuminating the night sky before our coach had even arrived at the gates.

"I should have warned you. With the changes the architect made, there is every possibility that she is taking the occasion to celebrate that as well as the reception for Sir James."

"The perfect situation for a thief to take advantage." A blunt reaction to my aunt's efforts.

"I am confident Munro has everything well in hand," I replied. "This is not his first soiree."

The entire front of the great old manor was illuminated from the main entrance up to the second-floor balconies. As a child growing up in that grand place, I had always loved all the candles and torches set about the grounds that had not been replaced by electric lights.

Our driver pulled to a stop at the end of the long line of coaches that had arrived ahead of us, with additional staff to assist the guests as they arrived.

I signaled him by tapping on the roof of the coach with my umbrella and asked him to take us round to the servant's entrance.

The driver pulled round to the east side of the manor and one of my aunt's servants scurried down the steps and opened the door.

"Evenin', Miss Mikaela, Mr. Brodie."

Even the servants' entrance had been transformed with barrels and crates of food, and the essence of some lavish meal that had been planned for the evening that filled the night air.

Brodie grimaced. "It occurs to me that your notion about making an excuse might have been far more pleasurable."

I tucked my arm through his. "Too late, and I do like your frowns almost as much as a smile."

"What are ye blathering about, woman?"

"Onward, Mr. Brodie, the party awaits."

Oh, my, I thought, as we reached the main hallway that led to the ballroom that had also been transformed.

It was possible that my aunt had outdone herself. Give her an occasion and that free spirit was capable of almost anything.

Tonight she had managed to recreate her version of Egypt, no doubt in honor of Sir James' travels. Or at least her version of that fascinating and ancient country where I had also traveled.

A panorama of the Valley of the Kings, recreated on screens, filled one wall of the ballroom complete with palm trees, a caravan of travelers making their way across the desert, and several Bedouin on a distant hillside waiting.

I was surprised that my aunt hadn't arranged for Cleopatra to make an appearance.

"Oh my," I commented as we made our way across the room to "Egypt." It was very much like the scenes recreated in museums and looked extremely familiar.

"What is it?" Brodie asked.

"It appears that my aunt has appropriated the background screens from the London Museum."

We crossed the "Nile" on what was in fact a stream of water redirected from a fountain in the garden room with a footbridge that had been constructed in the shape of one of the boats that could be found on that river, complete with a full-sized sail.

I peered over the *"railing"* as we crossed the bridge.

"What are ye looking for?" Brodie asked.

In consideration of my own personal experience on the River Nile, it was more a reflexive gesture— searching for crocodiles or the occasional body floating about.

I was relieved to see that my aunt hadn't appropriated one — crocodile that is, not a human body. Though, nothing would have surprised me.

"No bodies this evening," I replied.

"From yer adventures?" he took my hand and slipped my arm through his.

"An exciting few weeks, where I learned to expect almost anything," I explained.

"With Sir Redstone, I presume."

Now what was that about, I wondered?

My aunt was presently deep in conversation with a personal acquaintance— one of her ladies that she played cards with, and Sir James.

"Mikaela dear, and Brodie! Do come and greet our guest of honor," she called out.

Then, "Good heavens, Brodie," my aunt commented. "What have you done to yourself?"

I had attempted to persuade him to apply some of my face powder, however...

"A minor incident," he replied with a shake of his head. "Nothing more."

"You must take care, Brodie," she said quite affectionately. "Who else is there to retrieve Mikaela from her latest adventure?"

There were moments with my aunt. I turned to Sir James.

He was as I remembered him from our recent re-acquaintance, though somewhat older as I had observed that particular evening at the theater. However, still distinguished looking as I politely greeted him.

"My dear, Mikaela. It is good to see you once more. Lady Montgomery has been so kind to host this soiree this evening. And, Mr. Brodie," he added, almost as an afterthought.

Brodie merely nodded in that way of his. He was not one to draw attention to himself and preferred it that way.

"Yes, something about private inquiries that you make on behalf of clients, I seem to remember," Sir James commented. "Most interesting."

I was surprised that he even remembered. Or did he mean something else with the comment?

"They undertake those inquiries together," my aunt

explained. "Mikaela has become most proficient in resolving the most complicated cases and seems to enjoy scrabbling about in old buildings or going off to some place or another. With Mr. Brodie's assistance, of course."

"Fascinating," Sir James commented. "Something to occupy yourself, and of course such skills are necessary I suppose, with crime that seems to be everywhere."

Brodie and Sir James were of an even height but with a marked difference in their appearance. Though somewhat lean, Redstone held himself with that familiar bearing among those of the ton, what might be considered an elegant bearing.

Brodie's bearing was reserved, watchful, the evening coat stretched across wide shoulders and about well-muscled. And then there was his overlong hair, much in need of a trim, but which I had come to like very much.

"And you were once with the much-esteemed Metropolitan Police," Sir James commented.

Once more, Brodie merely nodded.

"Some of their inquiries have been most complicated and quite intriguing, even dangerous I must say." My aunt turned to me. "You must tell him about the illusionist and that poor girl who was murdered in the glass box. Dreadful situation."

"An adventure indeed, Miss Forsythe," Sir James suggested.

To anyone else Brodie might have seemed merely distracted, perhaps even bored with the direction of the conversation. However, I caught the slight narrowing of that dark gaze, his blackened eye notwithstanding.

Not distracted or bored, I thought. That razor-sharp mind was always at work. It had to be something else.

Brodie nodded, then turned to my aunt. "With your permission, Lady Montgomery, I will find Mr. Munro and see that everything... is in order."

By *"everything"* I knew from our earlier conversation that he referred to that *"perfect opportunity for thieves"* with guests arriving, servants coming and going, and the manor quite accessible to anyone else who might enter on an evening like this.

"London's finest, ever watchful," Sir James drily commented, which I found to be irritating and not to mention condescending. It was something I had not noticed in him during our travels years past.

Brodie merely nodded. "A particular... habit of mine. To make certain that there are no issues that might jeopardize the evening or her ladyship's guests."

With that he was gone, making his way through the guests that had gathered and those who were just arriving.

"An illusionist, the case must have been fascinating," Sir James said. "An unusual inclination for private inquiries into murders, a hobby perhaps?"

"Not at all," I replied. "There are many instances where certain crimes might go unsolved if not for our efforts."

He smiled. "I do remember from our mutual travel adventures your affinity for taking risks and going off on your own, which could be very dangerous."

"Balderdash," my aunt declared. "Oh, there is Sir Reginald, from the London Museum. I do owe a debt of gratitude to the man. He made it possible for me to acquire the panorama and the sarcophagi for the night, as well as some of the masks found in tombs.

"On loan, of course and with great care taken," she added. "It wouldn't do not to invite him after his generosity. Of course, everything must be returned after the evening. The damp weather can have a dreadful effect on them, quite different from Egypt." She laughed then. "It wouldn't do to have the mummies moldering inside the sarcophagi."

I didn't bother to explain that there were undoubtedly no mummies inside them as I had learned in previous visits to the museum and the antiquities department at university in my research for one of my novels. Those were very carefully preserved in glass cases.

With that, my aunt sailed off much like that replica of a boat on the Nile, across the bridge to where Sir Reginald stood looking very much the sort that one would find in a museum—distracted by everything about him and vaguely confused.

"I was somewhat surprised to learn that you had married," Sir James commented. "Although you were quite young at the time, you always seemed the sort that would go your own way, and now a novelist as well," he continued in a far warmer manner that might almost be considered flirtatious.

"I am grateful for the success, and it has allowed me to live independently."

"Independent from your husband as well?"

That certainly seemed a bold question. I ignored it and moved the conversation in a different direction.

"Your travels have kept you away for some time. What brings you back to London?"

I caught the slight lift of a brow.

"It was time, and I was curious to see if everything is the same as it was when I was last in England," he replied. "It seems that nothing has changed."

That seemed quite cryptic.

"There have been many changes the past few years," I replied. "We have more electric throughout the city as well as telephone service in most districts. Many of the older tenement buildings have been removed, with new ones planned for improved housing."

I thought of the tenement in Aldgate and what we had found there.

"The city is actively working with various charitable organizations to assist the poor," I continued. "It is said that very soon the underground rail system will be complete, with discussion about rail service under the channel connecting to France.

"There are advances in medical research as well," I added, thinking once more of Dr. Bennett and the procedures that had driven him to that tenement in Aldgate for some purpose.

"The workings of your mind were always most fascinating," he commented. "I remember that you particularly had a great compassion for the downtrodden. Most unusual, and not at all what someone might expect of someone... of title and wealth. However, things are never quite what they seem, are they?"

That seemed an odd thing to say, I thought as we traversed back across the "Nile," and I looked over the edge once more. I was grateful that my aunt hadn't acquired a creature to wander about, although I wouldn't have put it past her.

Templeton's iguana came to mind. Most certainly not the sort of creature that might be found in Egypt. Still, he would have made quite an interesting addition.

"Looking for something?" Sir James inquired. "Crocodiles perhaps?"

"No, bodies," I replied, thinking of that shared experience.

"A body?" he replied, almost as if he didn't remember it.

"I told my aunt about our adventure on the Nile."

"Yes..." he replied. "I had forgotten that sordid experience. A long time ago."

It had been quite unnerving for our fellow travelers. I then heard my name very nearby as we left the "Nile" and my sister approached along with Mr. Warren and Lily.

Linnie was thoroughly charmed by Sir James as she had heard most of my stories of my adventures or read about them in my novels.

"I have never traveled beyond France, but Mikaela most certainly has. Is it really as dangerous as everyone says that it is?"

"It can be..." he replied, then Mr. Warren joined the conversation. Perhaps interested in acquiring a distinguished author for his publishing company?

I left them to their questions about Sir James' travels, less interested than I thought I might be. There was something different from the man I had met and traveled with all those years before.

Of course, I was considerably younger then and everything seemed to have a sort of romantic aura about it— Egypt, the River Nile, and camping out in a tent in the desert.

I caught a glance from that striking blue gaze, a slight frown on Lily's face.

"He's right full of himself," she commented. "He's the sort the ladies at the 'Church' entertained. Thinks himself above others. Not at all like Mr. Brodie."

Quite observant of her.

"Have ye seen a lot of those places they talked about?" she asked, looking quite the young lady in a dress my sister had obviously selected for her.

"Several," I replied. There was of course, that other travel to the Isle of Crete... that quite ironically had included Brodie.

I suggested that we proceed to the dining room where supper had just been announced.

"Will there be strange things there?" Lily asked. "I heard one of the servants talk about unusual food."

Quite possibly I thought, considering my aunt's penchant for authentic details.

"There might be a goat's head, perhaps eel, roast poultry, lamb kofta meatballs served with sauce," I explained.

"A goat's head?" Lily replied with a frown. "But there's chicken? And maybe lamb?"

"Perhaps."

The expression on her face was adorable considering where she had lived previously— people with a penchant for goat's bellies. The frown was still there as she pulled me aside.

"I took this off one of the people who arrived to help the servants tonight." She handed me a lady's bracelet set with stones that were obviously quite valuable.

"He took it off the woman in the silver gown over by that statue."

The statue she pointed out was one of the sarcophagi. The lady was Mrs. Pomeroy, a friend of my aunt and currently in conversation with Sir James. Knowing Mrs. Pomeroy I was certain the bracelet was quite valuable.

"How did you get it?" I asked.

She shrugged. "I pinched it back."

My new role as guardian, sponsor, whatever one wanted to call it, was proving to be most interesting.

I supposed there were some who would have said that two wrongs did not make a right. However, I was not one of them.

While I didn't condone thievery, the fact that Lily had seen something that was wrong and chose to set it right made all the difference to me.

After all, I reasoned, considering where she came from—

not unlike Brodie's background, it would have been quite simple for her to say nothing at all, keep the bracelet, and then find an opportunity to sell it. She was, after all, quite resourceful.

She did, however, know the difference between right and wrong as I knew only too well, and I would not fault her for what she had done. Truth be known, I might very well have done the same thing.

"Come along," I told her as we approached the dining room. "I'll see that the bracelet is returned.

"A real goat's head?" she exclaimed.

The evening appeared to be a success for my aunt in introducing Sir James back into mainstream London Society.

"He is quite charming, don't you think," she asked as she found me in a game of cards in the Game Room where I was rapidly being outplayed.

Charming, yes, I thought, and... different from the man who had traveled with our group years before. However, I supposed that I was different as well.

Brodie had connected with Munro as I had suggested. He disappeared for a time, then reappeared, perhaps a little uncomfortable at such events, then later found Lily and myself in the Sword Room. My aunt's soiree, the goat's head, and card games having lost their earlier appeal, Lily had persuaded me to join her there.

"Who is winning?" Brodie asked as he found us, that dark gaze moving from one to the other.

"I got the last point," Lily smugly announced.

"That is still in question. Your mark was illegal," I replied as

I countered, parried, and then lunged with the rapier. The blunted tip caught her in the shoulder.

"My point, and match," I called out, bracing the sword before me, and taking my first rest since accepting her challenge.

Brodie crossed the floor and handed me his handkerchief. I was quite damp and my hair had come down. Not the most appealing appearance. He took the sword from me.

"A reminder to me not to challenge either one of ye. Are ye quite finished? The guests are startin' to leave. I thought ye might want to say good-evenin' to yer friend."

"Are ye goin' to tell 'im?" Lily asked then.

"Tell me wot?" Brodie asked with a look at me.

It appeared that she already had, more or less. I filled in the details regarding the bracelet.

"Can ye identify the man?" Brodie asked her.

She nodded. "Madame always had me keep a sharp eye out, especially with new ladies."

Brodie exchanged a look with me.

"Come along and point the fellow out," he told Lily, then paused before leaving.

He leaned in close, his fingers brushing my chin.

"Have I told ye that I like yer hair down like that?" That dark gaze, including the bruised one, darkened even more.

I felt my cheeks warm.

"Come along, miss," he told Lily.

Then they were gone to confront the thief.

In order to avoid a scene earlier, I had the bracelet returned to Mrs. Pomeroy by Mr. Symons, my aunt's head butler, with the explanation that the clasp must have come undone, and it was "found."

I followed downstairs and caught a glimpse of Munro who was in the process of removing the man in question.

I made our farewells to my aunt and sister, then approached Sir James.

He was in conversation with Sir Robert Crosswhite, a member of Parliament and a long-standing acquaintance of my aunt.

"You must attend now that you have returned," Sir Robert was saying. "Your father was a highly regarded member. Perhaps yourself as well in the future?"

"I appreciate the invitation," Sir James replied.

"Of course, and I will notify my people as well that you are my guest. One can't be too careful these days."

Sir Reginald appeared and politely reminded my aunt that his people would be back promptly in the morning to retrieve the panorama and the other Egyptian artifacts.

"Of course," she smiled.

When he had gone, assured by Mr. Munro that everything would be quite safe, I reminded my aunt, "Do be sure to return *both* sarcophagi to the museum, as well as all of the screens."

"Whatever do you mean, dear?" she replied appearing most innocent.

"They are on loan from the museum," I told her. "They expect everything to be returned."

"Of course, dear. But it had occurred to me that one of the sarcophagi might add a certain flair to the garden room for my ladies next luncheon..."

She was teasing, of course. At least I hoped that she was.


Brodie and I returned to the office on the Strand after leaving Sussex Square, and once again it occurred to me that the small space that was in fact no larger than my bedroom at the town-house was quite welcoming.

And of course, there was the adjacent room— the barest of accommodations to be certain, with outside plumbing down at the other end of the landing. Most would have thought it a dreadful inconvenience.

I did not. Perhaps it had to do with my travels to foreign places where accommodations were often limited. Or possibly it had something to do with the person who was there with me.

Brodie stoked up the fire in the stove with more coal and poured a bit of Old Lodge to warm the chill in the bones, as he called it.

I had left the notes Helen Bennett had given us for Dr. Bennett's second book as well as his first book, in the file cabinet after leaving Belgrave Square.

Was there something in either that might tell us the reason he had undertaken that basement office in Aldgate? And the reason he was murdered?

Or had it merely been his way of fighting back against the Society of Medicine and those who had censured his work? Then come upon by a street person, looking for coins or possibly some narcotic?

"Ye didna reprimand the girl for taking the bracelet," Brodie commented as he stepped from the adjacent room, struggling with the tie as he attempted to rid himself of it.

I set my glass on the desk, then went to him. I brushed his hands aside. He had pulled on one end of the tie, tightening rather than loosening it. I slowly worked it loose, then pulled one end from the knot, and removed it. His hand closed over mine.

"Some would say the lass deserved it," he added.

"I was quite a bit younger than Lily when I broke one of

my father's strict rules. That was before…" I hesitated, then let that part go.

No need to go back through difficult things, although Brodie was now well aware of most of the circumstances of my younger years.

"I had gone out to the kennels one afternoon when I was supposed to be in my room and let loose my favorite hound—Rupert."

"Ah. That explains a great deal about that smelly beast below that ye seem to have taken a fancy to."

He was right of course.

"I suppose my father was concerned that I might be hurt, going off like that. The hounds were used for hunting, and far outweighed either Linnie or myself at the time. But Rupert was special. I let him out then followed him on an adventure," I continued.

"Not the first of many, most certainly."

I ignored his sarcasm. "We were gone for some time, exploring the woods. I will admit that I became somewhat lost."

"Somewhat? Either ye were lost or ye were not."

I ignored that as well.

"However, I simply followed Rupert home. He knew precisely where he was going. My father was furious of course when we returned." I frowned at the memory.

"He beat Rupert horribly, even though I attempted to explain that he had brought me home, he had done nothing wrong, but simply obeyed me and had then done exactly what he was trained to do…"

"Lily is not a hound," Brodie pointed out. "She needs to know right from wrong."

"The point is," I continued, "that even though what she did might be seen as wrong, she did it for the right reason."

"Somethin' wrong fer the right reason?" Brodie took my hand and pressed it against his cheek.

"It amazes me the way yer thoughts work. A crime to undo a crime?" he suggested.

I was not about to let him get away with that.

"And you have done precisely the very same thing. Munro has told me..."

"I will have to speak with him about sharing stories with ye." He turned my hand and kissed the palm.

"Enough of yer stories, Mikaela Forsythe. There is nothing more to be done tonight. Leave this," he gestured toward the doctor's book and notes, "until the mornin'."

His hand then closed over mine and he led me to the adjacent bedroom.

We both undressed. I then turned off the electric and crawled between ice-cold bedcovers. And Brodie was there.

I moved toward his warmth, his arm going round my shoulders.

"Rupert, ye say? I should have known. Ye have a way of picking up stray things."

I smiled against his shoulder.

Indeed.

# Ten

"HOW DID you know where to go to find the office in Aldgate?" I asked, the doctor's notes and his book spread across the desk in front of me.

Brodie did not immediately reply from the adjacent bedroom. He eventually appeared dressed in his preferred trousers and sweater, his hair damp from a turn at the wash bowl. His eye did look somewhat better, although there were tinges of blue and green about the edges.

"Ye still insist on being part of this?"

Ah, so that was what had that dark gaze meeting mine, briefly, then looking away with what I do believe was a softly muttered curse.

I set my pen down on the desk. I had been going over my notes with the purpose of then putting them on the chalkboard, including the copy of that intercepted note I had managed to persuade from Alex Sinclair.

It was obviously written in some sort of code. The question was, what was it?

I had neatly organized Dr. Bennett's latest notes, according to the date at the top of each— the man was quite orderly in his thoughts, and now waited.

Brodie had been forthcoming in the matter, to a point. But I needed to know more. I continued to wait, then looked up and caught that dark gaze. He really was being quite obstinate this morning, which I had learned in the past required a different tactic.

I rose from behind the desk. I was not given to the usual woman's methods I had heard about from my sister, what I considered to be somewhat pathetic. Cajoling a man from some ill humor with what my sister referred to as *"feminine persuasion?"*

Not yet, at least.

Instead, I went to the coal stove where he had set the coffee pot earlier, seized his mug, battered and chipped as it was, and poured the steaming brew. I handed him the mug, then stood there where it was impossible to ignore me and waited. There was another curse between sips of coffee.

"Ye're like a dog with a bone," he muttered, which of course brought up images of Rupert with some disgusting object that he had managed to find in the back alleys off the Strand.

"Ye're not goin' to let this go, are ye?"

"We do owe it to *our* client to pursue every piece of information." I emphasized once more that Mrs. Bennett had engaged both of us.

"She hired ye to find her husband," he pointed out. "Ye've done that..."

"And to determine what happened to him," I emphasized. "I will not leave her without answers, and neither would you. She deserves that in the least," I continued. "And as for anything dangerous, I believe we have already had that conversation. You must get over that part, as I am not finished with this inquiry."

It did occur to me that I was poking the bear, so to speak. However, this was something that I was very determined about.

He set the empty mug down on the desk rather sharply and I wondered if it didn't crack further. There was only a small amount spilled over the edge. He then stalked— that was the only word for it —to the coat rack, retrieved his long coat, and put it on.

"I learned that a man resembling Soropkin arrived some weeks ago from the continent," he shared. "Through other sources I learned that he made inquiries about Dr. Bennett... regarding some *injury* that he apparently needed tending."

He had told me about the murder of Father Sebastian and the tailor.

"And the doctor's office in the tenement at Aldgate?" I prompted when it seemed he thought that was sufficient information.

"I was also given information from Mr. Brimley regarding a young boy who was horribly injured. The lad was poor and couldna afford the care he needed. It seems that particular care was beyond what Mr. Brimley or physicians at St. James could provide. It was suggested that the boy's father take him home..."

Home, to die. Too often a horrible fate.

However, it seemed Mr. Brimley, who provided care to the poor in the East End, was of a different mind. I knew quite well that he would not simply let the boy suffer and die.

"Brimley contacted Dr. Bennett," Brodie went on to share. "It seems that the good doctor had him take the boy to Aldgate as his methods would not have been approved otherwise."

"And he was he able to help the boy?" I asked.

Brodie nodded. "The procedures the doctor performed were successful. It seems that in time the boy will recover almost completely, with only a few small scars."

A boy who might otherwise have been left to die for want of treatment that Dr. Bennett had provided.

I wondered if it might be possible to see the boy. What might we learn from that?

"What of Soropkin? Is there no word where he might be?"

"It's as if the man is a ghost and Alex hasn't been able to decipher that intercepted message. What are ye thinkin'?" he asked as I gathered the notes and Dr. Bennett's book and put them in my travel bag.

"There could be something we might learn at the doctor's office in Aldgate. Some bit of information before Chief Inspector Abberline becomes involved."

"And ye intend to go back there."

"It could be beneficial to your part of the investigation as well," I replied. "And you would do the same."

I highly suspected that was where he was going. In the relatively short time we had been pursing inquiry cases, I had learned a thing or two about Angus Brodie.

"And I suppose if I left ye here, ye would simply go there on yer own."

"It is reasonable to share a cab and save the extra coach fare. And it might be helpful to have Mr. Brimley join us as he has considerable expertise in these matters."

These *matters* being the murder inquiries we had undertaken the past two years. He had been most helpful.

"I have already contacted him," Brodie replied.

It seemed that great minds thought alike. "Then we should leave immediately."

"I'll not wait for ye to go to Mayfair to change yer clothes into something more suitable."

"Not at all," I replied as I grabbed my wrap from the previous evening. "I'm quite ready." And moved past him to the door.

"In yer fine gown and slippers?"

"Do come along, Mr. Brodie."

I was already out the door and down the stairs to the street below.

We reached Aldgate to find that Mr. Brimley had already arrived. I caught the surprised expression on his face at my somewhat overdressed attire for such things as examining the scene of a murder. It seemed that satin and a bit of lace was somewhat overdone for such things.

Sir Avery had sent his people there late of the night, and as promised, the doctor's body had been removed, although the usual stench remained.

Even though the entrance to the basement office had been secured until a more extensive search of the clinic could be made, Brodie *"persuaded"* the door open. His skills from that previous life in Edinburgh did come in quite useful from time to time. I did need to have him show me how to do that.

Upon our previous visit, there had only been light from the street that had managed to find its way in through the heavily smudged street-level windows. We entered, then made our way into the adjacent room that had apparently served as some sort of examination room.

Brodie pushed the button beside the door, and the electric came on. I was surprised.

An oversight perhaps by the electric company with the building scheduled to be torn down? Or, had the doctor made arrangements for it to remain on?

That seemed the more likely possibility.

The sight before us was quite stark. Even though the doctor's body had been removed, the bloodstains remained just as we had found them, and I saw things that I had not noticed the night before.

There was a reclining chair on the other side of the room, much as in a gentleman's barber shop with a rolling steel table at one side, the same as that I had seen in the police mortuary.

There was a second steel table, however, it was toppled to the floor opposite as if it had been pushed over, with blood splattered across.

"There was a struggle here," Brodie observed as Mr. Brimley went about the room, carefully opening the doors of a cabinet, taking out bottles and jars to examine, removing lids and smelling the contents.

"There are some unusual substances not necessarily found in a physician's cabinet," Mr. Brimley commented. "A substantial amount of formaldehyde, and some other substance I not familiar with..."

"Ye'll be certain to take it to your shop," Brodie replied. "And perhaps learn something from that."

Brodie then turned that chair toward the meager light that spilled in from the street.

"There is a residue here," he told the chemist who immediately joined him while I proceeded to make my own inspection.

Not that I thought myself equal to Brodie or Mr. Brimley, however I looked for things from my admittedly somewhat limited experience, while they approached from a different perspective.

They inspected the "residue" on the chair, their heads bent together, one tall, the other substantially shorter.

"There might be somethin' there," Brodie commented.

Mr. Brimley then took an envelope from his coat pocket, along with a small knife.

He scraped a portion of the residue into the envelope and then pocketed it as Brodie continued his inspection, kneeling on the floor.

"What do ye make of this, Mr. Brimley?"

Brodie held aloft a rather unusual looking bladed instrument, that drew Mr. Brimley's attention.

The chemist adjusted his glasses as he inspected the instrument.

"With what I found in that cabinet, it would seem that the good doctor was not only treating the usual ailments, but performing surgeries as well. There are some fine instruments that could be found in a hospital, or a morgue for examination of a body."

There were also books. I discovered, three to be exact. None were authored by the doctor, however, and all three were written in Latin, and some other language that was vaguely familiar, and included drawings.

One was extremely old and there was no front piece as usually found in published books, my own included, that at least contained an author's name.

The last one was more of a manuscript that had not yet been published. A good deal of text was also in Latin. In several places was what appeared to be Greek and Egyptian text.

I frowned, French and Latin were the extent of my studies.

"Have ye found somethin'," Brodie asked. I looked up.

"It appears to be an old manuscript," I replied. "It's written in Latin and makes references to Egyptian text. It appears to be made of parchment."

"Latin ye say?"

I had caught Mr. Brimley's interest as well.

"I was able to read that much in the first few pages."

I was forced to admit that I had other interests when at my lessons that had not included ancient Egyptian. Mr. Brimley, however, was substantially more accomplished, no doubt due to his early medical education.

"It is a Latin translation and includes several references in what appears to be some form of Egyptian script. Fascinating," he added. "However, beyond my abilities."

Fascinating and confusing. It was not surprising that Dr. Bennett had a knowledge of Latin. That would have come from his formal education as a physician. However, references and writings in some other text? What could that mean?

I thought of Sir Reginald, who had provided the Egyptian panorama and sarcophagi on loan from the museum. He had spent years exploring Egypt and was responsible for the main exhibit that was there now, along with artifacts.

"I know someone who may be able to assist with this. It could tell us something important about what Dr. Bennett was working on that the Society disapproved of so strongly."

What might the notes for his next book, also be able tell us?

I carefully closed the manuscript. As I did a piece of paper fell from among the pages to the floor. I picked it up.

It was very fine note paper, the sort that someone might keep in their desk to write invitations, or responses to someone over an invitation received. Or possibly at a physician's office, when writing to someone who had lost a loved one?

*My dearest wife,*

*You have always been my champion,*
*and believed in me when others did not...*

It was here where the doctor had obviously paused, ink from the pen forming a puddle that was now dry, before he had continued with a note he obviously never had the opportunity to give her. And the next line...

*I do what I must now do, to keep you safe.*

I looked up at Brodie.

"Is there a date on it?"

I shook my head and handed the note to him.

"It would appear that the doctor was about to do something that might have gone against his ethics, his profession, or at the least, the Society of Medicine."

"To keep her safe? From a threat?" I suggested.

"So it would seem. There was obviously a struggle here before the doctor was murdered."

Brodie was thoughtful as he scanned the room, the overturned table, the instruments scattered about, and those blood stains.

A threat? For what purpose? And another piece of the puzzle for which there was no answer. Yet.

I carefully tucked the manuscript into my travel bag, along with the note. It might be of some comfort to Helen Bennett. Mr. Brimley had made his own notes about his observations which he handed to Brodie as we left.

The ride to Mayfair, after leaving Mr. Brimley, was a silent one. We were both lost to our own thoughts regarding what we had learned with our visit to that hidden office.

I wanted very much to know what the text in that manuscript meant, while Brodie needed to return to the Agency with what he had found at the murder scene, along with Mr. Brimley's notes and my discovery of the manuscript.

"I would like to have Sir Reginald inspect the manuscript," I told him, breaking the silence.

"He's very knowledgeable and he may be able to tell us something important."

Brodie agreed. "I will explain to Sir Avery."

We arrived and the driver waited for him as I had stepped down from the coach in front of the townhouse.

"Ye will take care and not go off without my knowing."

Under any other circumstances, I might have objected.

"I do want to call on Helen Bennett."

"The note?"

I nodded. "She should have it. It may bring some comfort that his thoughts were of her."

There was something more, but he obviously decided against it.

"Soropkin is somehow involved. He's a verra dangerous man..."

"I'll be careful," I assured him. "Careful as a church mouse."

"See that ye do. Until we know what this is about..."

"I can take care of myself," I reminded him.

He gently touched my chin.

"That is wot concerns me."

When he had gone, I made use of the shower compartment

in the bathroom, a recent convenience that we had discovered had additional benefits...

Afterward, I placed a telephone call to Sussex Square and learned that Sir Reginald had already returned with museum staff and retrieved the panorama along with the two sarcophagi.

"*As if I could not be trusted to have them returned,*" my aunt commented, somewhat indignant.

I then inquired about Lily and was told that she was in the library with her latest tutor— she had somehow managed once more to send the most recent one off in a fit of despair, declaring that she was unmanageable and obviously quite ignorant.

"*Can you imagine?*" my aunt said with a chuckle.

I thought a diversion might be in order and decided to take Lily with me to the museum. I assured my aunt that it would be an excellent learning experience.

For her part, Lily was much in favor of anything that might free her from the drudgery of studies. Most definitely a girl after my own heart.

My aunt arranged for her driver to bring Lily to Mayfair, and then take us to the museum.

I then placed a call to the museum. I was informed that Sir Reginald was in the Egyptian Hall presently overseeing the installation of *several items.*

I could only guess they included the panorama screens and the sarcophagi retrieved from Sussex Square. He was known to be a perfectionist and it seemed that he would be there for several hours. Perfect.

"Museum?" Lily commented as we departed Mayfair together.

"There is a great deal to learn at a museum," I explained. "About history, different places, and people." I paused.

I was definitely not making the right impression. And, I had to admit, at fourteen years of age, or as near as Lily knew her age to be, I would very likely have had the same reaction.

When confronted with boredom, it was best to appeal to what interested someone, and in Lily's case...

"There are a great many weapons there as well," I added. "Early firearms, spears and staffs, and swords."

She did have a particular fascination with swords, and score one in favor of myself as I saw her interest piqued.

"Swords?"

We found Sir Reginald in the midst of the Egyptian collection with a team of assistants. His shirtsleeves rolled back to his elbows and his face gleamed with perspiration as he gave directions to the young men much like a field commander shouting instructions.

"No, no! That is not it at all! The screens must be in a specific order to complete the scene. It is quite obvious. Pay attention to what you are doing!"

Perhaps not the best time to call on him, however time was of the essence and the attendant at the entrance to the museum had informed us that Sir Reginald was due to depart for his next trip abroad within a fortnight.

Lily was immediately drawn to the collection of ceremonial staffs. I did hope that she didn't decide to try one out as I approached Sir Reginald.

"Yes, yes, what is it now?" he demanded without turning around when I asked to speak with him.

"I would have spoken with you last evening," I explained.

He then turned with that slightly myopic gaze over the top of his glasses and stared at me.

"Lady Forsythe..."

"A moment of your time, if you please," I explained, and then added, "and your expertise."

He turned back to the task at hand and shouted at another one of the assistants who looked quite flustered.

"I've come across a manuscript that I believe may contain references in a language I'm not familiar with," I explained. "It looks very much as if it might be Egyptian, and since you are the foremost authority..."

Never let it be said that I am above using flattery.

"I was hoping you might take a look and see what you can make of it."

"Egypt," he replied with what could only be a mesmerized smile as he watched the screens of the panorama set in place.

"Land of mystery and ancient kingdoms." Then the spell seemed to have left him, at least for the time being. His demeanor immediately changed.

"Of course, no doubt some relic from your travels, I suspect? I understand that you have been to Alexandria as well as the Valley of the Kings. How may I assist?"

I glanced over at Lily to make certain she wasn't dismantling the stand that displayed the Egyptian staffs. I then opened my travel bag and retrieved the manuscript and laid it atop a glass enclosed display case that contained several pieces of Egyptian artifacts.

"Papyrus?" Sir Reginald immediately noted.

"So it would seem," I replied. "Part of it is in Latin which I was able to decipher. However there are other references that appear to be Egyptian."

"Do stop what you are doing, before you damage the piece!" he shouted past me to the assistants who struggled with the latest screen in the panorama.

"It is so difficult to get good help," he added. "Most frustrating. They simply do not understand the incredible importance of our exhibits and the artifacts we have collected."

He turned to me then. "Yes, quite. You have a question about a manuscript?"

Sir Reginald studied several pages, his lips mouthing the words in Latin, the best that I had been able to determine, using the opposite end of his pen to lift the pages so not to touch with his fingers and soil them.

"Hmmm. Yes, Egyptian to be certain..." he turned another page. "But which dialect? That is the question. See here, it is not what one of your experience might expect. There are not the usual characters that we are most familiar with from our explorations."

He pointed to a glass encased jar nearby that was covered with hand-painted images of a bird and cat.

"See there, that is a perfect example of hieroglyphics, however..." He continued to study several more pages of text.

"Perhaps Demotic script, or possibly Coptic. I would say, by the structure of this, similar to others I have seen, that this could possibly be from around the eleventh century— B.C. that is. See here, obviously Greek letters as well, and the words are run together.

"And this sort of script is seen primarily in administrative or official documents and treatises that have been discovered— most interesting, and the Latin text refers to it. It seems to describe some sorts of procedures."

Procedures? That caught my attention.

"Most unusual, and rare. How did you come by it?" he then asked.

That was a conversation for another time, that didn't include discussion about murder.

"Might you be able to translate it?" I inquired. "It's important."

"Most interesting," he went on. "Of course it will take some time..."

I pointed out that it was regarding a most urgent matter.

"I could have something for you..." He was once more distracted by the manuscript.

"Sir Reginald?" I reminded him.

"Oh yes, quite. I could have something for you perhaps tomorrow, if you will contact the museum in the morning..."

That would have to do. In the meantime, I wanted very much to read Dr. Bennett's book as well as those notes he had been making for his next book.

I made arrangements to contact Sir Reginald the following morning, then turned to gather my bag. It was quite cumbersome with the book, the notes, and the revolver I usually carried at Brodie's insistence.

The bag tumbled to the floor of the hall, Dr. Bennett's notes scattering about as Lily arrived, quite excited. She stooped down to help retrieve the notes.

"One of the attendants said as how some of those staffs are over two thousand years old. Two thousand years! I canna imagine. The 'Church,' in Old Town, was only three hundred years old. The ladies were always complainin' that there was no plumbing after they finished with their customers. Did they have plumbing two thousand years ago?"

She managed to shuffle the loose notes together. We did need to have a conversation about the things she shared in public places.

"Wot's this, Miss Mikaela?" She held up one of the pieces of paper that had been in my bag.

It was the copy of that note the Agency had intercepted

and had been unable to decipher. She seemed particularly fascinated by it.

"It looks like some sort of code with all those letters and numbers." She handed it back to me. "Is it part of the inquiry ye're makin'?"

I distracted her with a reminder of swords that were displayed in another part of the great hall.

That took us to the Medieval Hall where there were several displayed, including several from France after various campaigns— we never did seem to get along, although the Conqueror, an ancestor, had been French. Norman actually according to my aunt. There was also a particularly well-preserved Crusader sword.

"The knife Mr. Munro gave ye is more practical," Lily commented.

"I believe, in the past, the object was to engage one's opponent at a greater distance than that of a knife to get an advantage and strike a fatal blow," I explained.

She nodded. "Slice off an arm or the head, I s'pose."

Quite graphic, but to the point.

We spent a bit of additional time exploring other collections from Egypt as well as India, Africa, and the Pacific Islands, along with the different weapons for each that had been collected.

Upon leaving the museum we found a driver and gave him the address at Sussex Square.

Lily was unusually quiet when she normally would have had a barrage of questions, and we were well on our way across the city to my aunt's residence.

"The first letter makes no sense," she said staring out of the coach. "But if you look at the next ones, there is a pattern," she commented quite unexpectedly.

"I beg your pardon," I replied.

"That's it, miss!" she said with a great deal of excitement. "It's a code, and not all that difficult." She grinned.

"It's not complicated and not all that different from the messages the ladies used to send back and forth to each other regarding the men they entertained at the Church. They used to let each other know who paid well and who might try to get away with... Well, you know."

Having been at the "Church" in question, I did know quite well. However that didn't explain what she was talking about.

"Ye just have to figure out the sequence, then when it repeats, the words are there. The note that fell out of yer bag. It took me a while, but I figured it out."

I stared at her. She seemed to think that she had found the code to decipher that message. This from a girl who had been a lady's maid in a brothel and didn't know how to read!

I immediately signaled for the driver to change direction and take us to the office on the Strand.

# Eleven

WE WORKED TOGETHER. Lily read off the letters and numbers in that note and I then wrote them on the blackboard in precisely the same order.

It was brief, there was only one row, but it meant something to someone, intercepted by a man in Luxembourg who worked for the Agency and had paid dearly for it.

In her former life in the brothel, one of Lily's responsibilities was to keep track of letters, notes, and bills that came into the "Church." In addition there was some sort of code the ladies used that not only warned which customers paid and which did not, but also apparently rated the men according to... the *deed*, as she put it.

Lily had learned to decipher the messages in those notes, but I suspected it was more than merely clever observation. She was obviously quite gifted in ways we were only beginning to discover— her awareness of things, and her ability to learn something and remember it in short order with just a glance, much like a photograph.

I laughed at her comment— that men might be rated

according to how well they *"performed."* I did wonder if the ladies awarded points or some other method.

Most interesting.

"Miss?" she drew my attention back to the task at hand.

It was time to put to use the sequence she was certain would determine what the message was.

"Please continue," I told her. "Let's see what you have."

"The letters dinnae make sense at first," she began. "But the first one is usually important in a message, right?"

"The first letter is an X," she pointed out. "And the next three letters make no sense either, T, R, and another X."

I listened intently.

"If ye follow the number of places— then ye come to the letter 'A.' The first letter in the message is an 'A.' Then four more, and the next letter is L, followed by..." she counted off the same number once more, "another L."

A-L-L. The word *all*.

Had she actually discovered the key to the coded message?

Using the same sequence, I applied it to the remainder of the message.

When the next letters had been revealed I stood back from the board to view what had emerged. The letters I had circled all ran together.

*all i np l ace*

It was now merely a matter of separating the words in that string of letters.

*All- in- place*

Something was *"in place!"*

I looked over at Lily. It did seem that she had in fact deciphered the message so far. Clever girl.

Her brow wrinkled. "And then, there is the numbers. If ye apply the same number of places..."

The sequence of four numbers then the next one revealed is a one, then an eight, followed by another one and then a two, using that same sequence.

*1-8 and then 1-2*

And the final letters that emerged:

*P—A—R—L—S*

Was it some sort of shorthand writing that the person it had been intended for would understand from previous messages?

P-A-R-L-S? Could it possibly mean Parliament? But then the additional letter— S, made no sense.

Brodie had once referred to my notes written in shorthand as *"that gibberish that no one was able to understand."*

He had, however, later admitted that it did appear to be quite useful when I was able to quote a comment a suspect had made. One that I had quickly written down that had proven useful in our inquiry case at the time.

He had been sufficiently impressed, contrary to the saying *"one couldn't teach an old dog new tricks."* He hadn't been particularly amused by that reference.

I heard the sound of steps at the landing. Brodie entered the office, covered with a dusting of snow upon his coat and hair.

"Mr. Cavendish said ye returned some time ago," he

commented as he immediately went to the stove to warm his hands.

"Were ye able to learn anythin' at the museum?"

"We deciphered the code in the message!" Lily excitedly replied. "That is the right word, miss?"

"That is the word," I replied.

Brodie looked over, obviously somewhat surprised to find her there.

"I thought a visit to the museum might be interesting for her," I explained. "And Sir Reginald may be able to assist with the notes Dr. Bennett had. As for the code..."

"Wot are ye talking about?"

"It seems that Lily has been able to decipher the message the Agency intercepted; the one I had a copy of, thinking that I might be able to assist with it," I reminded him.

"It appears that Lily has figured it out."

"Wot do ye believe ye have discovered?"

By his tone it was obvious that he was skeptical, and quite possibly merely indulging the both of us.

"Actually, it was Lily who discovered the code sequence and then deciphered the message."

"I didna mean to interfere," she started to explain. "I happened to see it, and it was just there— the way the letters stood out. It happens that way sometimes."

"Ye didna interfere," Brodie assured her, then with a look over at me. "That had already taken place. Now, Miss Lily," he told her, "show me what ye have found."

A smile spread across her face as she went to the blackboard and explained the pattern she had discovered.

"Miss Mikaela helped," she added and pointed to the message that had emerged using the pattern she had discovered.

Brodie studied the board, that dark gaze narrowed in

concentration.

"It seems to mean that something important is to happen," Lily pointed out the obvious.

He continued to study the message.

"But we were only able to figure out part of it. Then there are the numbers ye see, and more letters. They must mean somethin'."

He read the numbers aloud. "An address, or possibly something else."

"One and then an eight," I repeated, then, "Could the one and eight actually be the number eighteen?"

Eighteen. What did that mean?

"The eighteenth?" Was that it? If so, then the next two numbers, one and two?"

"Something is supposed to happen on the eighteenth of December?"

Brodie looked at me. "Verra possible."

And today was the fourteenth of December.

"That could mean that something is planned for four days from now."

"Ye did well," he told Lily. "It would seem that ye have found something verra important." And then with a look over at me.

"The rest of it is for us to determine."

The question was: *What* was to happen and *where*? And what did the rest of those letters mean?

"I do not trust the telephone service," Brodie announced. "A call often passes through too many hands. Ye never know who might be listenin'."

Such as those who might find the information we'd uncovered and pass it to someone else? But what did it mean?

While I thought of the usual conversations I had on the telephone— responding to an invitation, a call to the cab service, or recent conversations with my sister or Lily about various things, I realized quite clearly his meaning.

It did seem that new inventions, marvelous as they were, also brought new and perhaps dangerous possibilities.

He had placed a call to Alex Sinclair and asked for him to meet us at the office on the Strand. He mentioned only that it was important, nothing more.

It was very near an hour later when Alex arrived, quite soaked through from the weather, his cheeks and ears reddened from the cold.

"Have you learned something?" he managed to ask from between teeth that chattered.

I handed him a cup of hot coffee with a bit more something else to warm him.

"Oh, this is quite wonderful, Miss Forsythe," he said after taking a sip. He glanced past me to the blackboard.

"Oh, I say, what have you there?" His gaze scanned the original message. "This looks very much the same as the message our people intercepted in Luxembourg."

"The same," Brodie replied.

"And the rest of this?" Alex asked.

"The decoded message," I explained. "Or at least part of it. Something is in place to happen on December eighteenth."

He stared incredulously at it. "How? I wasn't able to decipher any of it with my machine."

"It was easy," Lily spoke up even though I had cautioned her to let Brodie discuss the matter with Alex. She went to the board and went through the sequence that she had discovered.

"Incredible," Alex replied, then looked at her. "And you saw the sequence when you first looked at it?"

She nodded. "It happens sometimes. I look at something, like the word puzzles, and the letters just seem to be in the right place."

"Incredible."

That was two "incredibles" in the last few minutes.

"The question now is what does it mean..." Brodie concluded. "Sir Avery must be made aware of this, and we need to figure out what is to happen on the eighteenth of the month, and where."

"Have you been able to find anything more about Soropkin?" Alex asked.

Brodie shook his head. "I have people searching for him, but... no. However, Mikalea may be able to provide some information that she has uncovered that could be useful."

"I have the curator of the museum looking over Dr. Bennett's notes and an old manuscript we found in Aldgate," I explained when Alex looked over at me.

"Much of it appears to be in some Egyptian dialect. It may provide some insight to what he was working on and the reason he was murdered. And we do know that Brodie has learned that Soropkin was supposedly seen in Aldgate before he disappeared."

"You believe there's a connection?" he asked Brodie.

"We may very well know more tomorrow when Mikaela learns what was in the manuscript the doctor had in his possession when he was murdered."

"I'll let Sir Avery know about the code," Alex replied. "He may have some thoughts on it as well. And you will let us know what you are able to learn tomorrow?"

"Of course," I assured him.

Lily had been quiet after explaining how she had deciphered the code, with a great deal of interest it seemed, in our conversation with Alex.

"Murder?" she exclaimed.

Hmmm. An explanation was needed, albeit a very brief one.

"A case that Mr. Brodie is working on."

"And that message has somethin' to do with it?"

"Perhaps." I gathered my bag, then went to retrieve my long coat.

"Where are we goin'?" she excitedly asked.

"You are going to return to Sussex Square," I replied. She instantly pulled a face.

"You have given us a valuable clue," I continued. "Without your assistance Mr. Brodie might have gone on for days. It was important and we are both most grateful. However..."

"There is that word again," she grumbled. "Everyone uses it — however."

"However," I began again, "your education is very important."

"Wot do I need with more education? Mr. Brodie never had any education."

"Not true."

His education had come from the streets and what he picked up along the way, pushing himself up out of the gutters as he once told me.

"He acquired his education along the way, and so must you."

"If I get this education, then I could be of more help to ye?" she replied.

Clever girl.

"You could achieve a great many things."

"And maybe work with ye and Mr. Brodie? That could be worth the aggravation of learnin' how to speak proper and act like a lady like Miss Lenore told me."

Aggravation. I had to agree with her, however...

We made our way to the alcove on the street below.

I had Mr. Cavendish summon a cab for her, with instructions for the driver that he was to take her directly to Sussex Square with no stops along the way— not that I didn't trust her, and there would be extra fare in it for him when they arrived. I was confident that my sister would see the matter taken care of.

With Lily safely departed, Brodie was off as well, to see someone— the man in German Town who claimed to have seen Soropkin.

Before Brodie could object, I had Mr. Cavendish summon another cab. There was someone I wanted to see. It might very well be important.

Mr. Brimley was most accommodating when I arrived and made my request.

"The woman lives in Stepney. She lost her husband last year and the boy has done his best to support the family since." He shook his head.

"A dreadful accident. One of the worst I've ever seen, and the lad needed far more care than I could provide."

I then asked if he thought I might visit with the boy, that it might be important to our investigation since Dr. Bennett was able to help the boy.

"Mr. Brodie already paid a visit and took a few boxes of

food to help them get by until the boy can return to work." He eyed me sharply. "Did he tell you to come here?"

I wouldn't lie to him, as he had become a good friend and most important to our inquiry cases.

"I thought so," he answered his own question when I was hesitant. "He worries for you, miss. After that first case."

"That was very near two years ago and I am quite well recovered, as you know. However, I might be able to help him with this."

"I'll probably regret this, what with his temper, most particularly where you are concerned…"

He shook his head.

"You are too bold for your own good, miss. I don't know of another woman who would take it upon herself to help solve a murder case. And I suppose you don't want me to mention this to Mr. Brodie."

That would happen soon enough, if I was to learn anything with the visit. If not, then it didn't matter.

The boy, Ethan, his mother and two sisters lived in a flat on Leman street, in Stepney, near the sugar refinery. In spite of his young age at twelve years, Ethan had worked in the warehouse next to the refinery, loading sacks of sugar daily onto wagons that then made deliveries across the city. Until a dreadful accident.

In spite of that poor East End of London, their flat, when we arrived, was spotlessly clean with work tables set up for Ethan's mother and sisters. They took in needlework for some of the better shops in order to make ends meet.

Mr. Brimley introduced me upon our arrival. It seems that he had been there before to check up on the boy after Dr. Bennett saved his life.

Ethan's mother, Agnes, was surprisingly young, perhaps

only a few years older than myself, although her features were careworn. Still, there was a warm smile for Mr. Brimley, and a courteous nod toward myself.

He had brought brown bread sweetened with molasses, a bottle of medication for Ethan to help him sleep at night, and fresh bandages.

My introduction to Ethan was most unsettling, and something I would not forget.

He had been injured in a fire at the refinery where he had gone with one of the workers to pick up a load of sugar. There was a fire in the refinery that quickly spread.

Ethan had been unable to escape. Trapped by the fire, he had been badly burned on his hands and face as he tried to help put out the fire. He was bandaged about both hands, with more bandages about his head. He was also bandaged about the middle of his body.

"The doctor said that in time there won't hardly be any scars to his face," Mr. Brimley whispered. "He used skin from the lad's back to replace the burnt skin on his face. I've heard of it, but never known of it here in England.

"It seems that the wounds accept the new skin because it's from the same person," he continued. "Then, the bandages are applied with a salve that the doctor provided. He gave me a list of the ingredients so that I could mix it at the shop. Hopefully it will be successful. The methods are old, however, and not without risk."

"What sort of risk?" I asked.

"If not cared for properly, like any wound, the new tissue could begin to die."

I could only imagine the horror of that possibility.

"I will see the boy through," he assured me.

I approached the cot where Ethan lay, still weak even though it had been almost three weeks since the accident.

I could see skin on his neck beginning to heal, without the gruesome damage left behind by fire that I had seen when in Edinburgh with Brodie.

A miracle indeed, I thought, as Ethan nodded. "I canna stand so good as yet, miss."

I assured him that wasn't necessary as Mr. Brimley explained the reason I was there. He made it sound more like a social call to put the family at ease.

"I work with Mr. Brodie," I explained. "He told me about your accident and the fire. I was hoping you might be able to tell me about Dr. Bennett."

The boy's eyes lit up. "He fixed me real good. I can use me hands, and he said that in time there won't be any scars on me face."

"It was terrifying," his mother put in. "They brought his back here and I swear I was certain that he was...

"Mr. Brimley heard of Dr. Bennett and contacted him. Then we took Ethan to Aldgate, not one of them hospitals. I didn't understand, but the doctor assured us that he could take care of Ethan there."

"Did you see anyone else while you were there?" I asked. "Possibly someone else who had come to see the doctor?"

She shook her head. "I didn't see no one else, miss. The doctor was there all alone. He had to leave after he saw to Ethan and I stayed there until he returned. Then he sent us home with my boy all bandaged up like you see him. And in the time since, he's already started to heal."

"Did Dr. Bennett mention anything about the treatment he gave Ethan?"

"He said that we shouldn't tell anyone, that it might mean trouble for him. According to Mr. Brimley, we wouldn't have gotten the same from other doctors and Ethan would have died."

"Is there anything else you can tell me? Something you saw or something that happened while you were there but perhaps thought nothing of?"

"It was just me and Ethan with the doctor," she replied. "He was unconscious most of the time." She hesitated.

"What is it?"

She looked at Mr. Brimley, uncertain. He nodded. "You can tell her."

"There was a man, showed up at the door of the doctor's office."

"What did he look like?"

"Didn't get a good look; he wore a long coat with his hat pulled low and a neck scarf wrapped about 'im. But I did see the bandages, like my boy here. 'im and the doctor spoke some, then he left real sudden.

"Seein' how the doctor helped my boy and all, I figured it was another patient who was injured. It didn't seem important." She looked from me to Mr. Brimley.

"That's fine, Agnes," he assured her. "And it looks to me as if you are taking good care of the boy."

She nodded. "'im and the girls are all I have."

"Apply that salve when you change the bandages. I'll come by again in a few days," he told her.

She laid a tentative hand on his arm. "I can't pay you right now wot with Ethan not working. Everythin' the girls and I earn goes for food."

"Don't you worry about that, Agnes." He patted her hand. "You just take care of the boy."

I wished Ethan well in his recovery and thanked his mother

for speaking with me. What I had learned about the surgery he received was fascinating. What might that mean for others badly injured?

"I would like to help them," I told Mr. Brimley as we left.

"The rent is most important now. Mr. Brodie already took care of that for the month. But next month..."

It wasn't the first time Brodie had intervened on behalf of some family in the East End.

"I'll see that you have the money for next month when you return to see to Ethan, and for your care of him as well."

We walked the short distance to the main thoroughfare where we were eventually able to find a driver.

"It's but a drop in a *bucket*, miss, for them that live in these places," he said as we returned to his shop.

"A very large *bucket*," I replied, it being obvious with so much poverty in the East End. "And yet you stay, when you might be able to set up your shop in another part of London and make a decent living."

"And you might refuse to take inquiry cases for those such as the good doctor who only wanted to help those like Ethan."

"What is to be done?" I then asked. But I knew— changes. There were changes taking place, as I had told Sir James. However, it was painfully slow, and seemed almost impossible at times.

"I'll take fresh bandages and a box of food to Ethan and his mother, and the girls. And I suspect that you will find the murderer who killed the good doctor."

I thought a great deal about what I had learned in my visit with Ethan and his mother.

It was apparent from what she told us that Brodie might very well not be aware of the man she had seen— a man dressed in a long coat with a scarf, his hat worn low that didn't quite conceal heavy bandages about his face. Another injury that the doctor had helped the man with?

After seeing Mr. Brimley back to his shop, I then had the driver take me to the office on the Strand.

It was very nearly evening, fog wrapping around lamp posts as the rain set in when I arrived. There was a light in the window of the office at the second-floor landing.

"Mr. Brodie returned some time ago," Mr. Cavendish greeted me.

Rupert appeared, promptly sat at my feet, and nudged my hand. I had been somewhat remiss recently in bringing him some of Mrs. Ryan's sponge cakes or scones.

"There was a bloke 'round earlier, tall, like any working man in this part of London. But there was somethin' about 'im, the way he carried himself. Didn't seem right," he continued. "And he seemed most interested in the office, kept lookin' this way. The hound set up quite a ruckus.

"I mentioned it to Mr. Brodie. Thought he should know, with you bein' here by yerself from time to time."

What might that mean, I thought. Merely one of the people on the street? Someone looking for work or possibly a handout? Or, perhaps someone Brodie had spoken with, one of his "sources?"

I thanked him and headed for the stairs.

Brodie looked up from the desk as I entered the office. There was that frown, and I fully expected a comment about being out "alone" again, which I had not. At least not the entire afternoon.

I removed my neck scarf and coat.

"Miss Lenore called round to let ye know that Lily arrived safely back at Sussex Square after yer visit to the museum." He set the pen down rather sharply and I sensed the question that came next.

"Several hours ago."

After calling on Ethan and his mother, I was not of a mind to hear his usual objections about taking myself off alone. It was one of those things that needed a conversation between us.

I had been "taking myself off," as he put it for some time in my travels, however I supposed that Brodie had a point— a point my sister had also made a few weeks earlier when I had casually mentioned that he seemed somewhat adamant about my "independent nature" as he put it.

*"He's only concerned for your welfare,"* Linnie had explained. *"Quite understandable under the circumstances, there is now the two of you."*

The circumstances being our inquiry cases that had admittedly been somewhat dangerous from time to time, and the recent change in our relationship that I was adjusting to.

*"I would think that you might appreciate that, someone who cares deeply for you,"* she had continued. *"I never had that, at least not before. You must learn to compromise."*

"That" referring to her marriage that had ended the year before, and the dreadful circumstances that had taken her to that point.

"Mr. Brimley was good enough to accompany me to Stepney. I met with Ethan and his mother."

There, I thought, *compromise.*

"When you explained that you learned Dr. Bennett had treated the boy's injuries, I thought there might be... something else that could be important."

I was not usually at a loss for words. But the visit with Ethan had deeply affected me, far more than I had anticipated. I went to the stove to warm my hands.

I had seen injured children before in the course of our inquiries, some quite seriously. But Ethan had been so very brave, and to think the boy might have been permanently maimed and scarred.

"To see him... the wounds were obviously quite severe. If not for Dr. Bennett..." I was rattling on as Brodie would have called it, quite out of character for me.

I heard the scrape of his chair across the floor then felt those strong hands, gentle on my shoulders. I turned and he pulled me into his arms.

"It would seem that Dr. Bennett very well may have discovered new ways to help those injured like Ethan," I went on, soaking the shoulder of his shirt as the tears came, and I never cried.

"Why would someone want to harm the doctor...?" The rest of it caught in my throat, and then in that way that he knew what I was thinking.

"Fear perhaps, professional jealousy," Brodie suggested.

The cold knot that I'd carried back from Stepney slowly eased.

When had I come to need that? How had I convinced myself that I didn't need such things?

"Ye're shaking," he said then. "Have ye eaten anythin' today? Ye know how ye are when ye dinnae eat."

I shook my head. He handed me his handkerchief, then went to the door and called down to Mr. Cavendish with a request to have food sent over from the Public House.

The food and another dram of my aunt's whisky helped considerably as I told Brodie of my visit to the museum that morning and the hope that Sir Reginald might be able to tell us something important once he translated Dr. Bennett's notes and that manuscript.

"Aye, it could be useful."

I held out my glass for another dram.

"He's quite certain now that the writings in the papyrus are Coptic. It's a very old Egyptian dialect, but he seemed confident that he could translate it."

Somewhere along the way, Brodie took the empty glass from my hand and mentioned that it was quite late.

I rose from my chair with the intention of making my way to the adjacent room. However, at last count, there had been at least two drams of my aunt's whisky. Or was it three?

I wobbled slightly and Brodie was there to unwobble me. One arm went about my waist, the other under my legs and he carried me into the bedroom.

He set me on the edge of the bed, then began to unlace my boots. He removed one, then the other.

"Ethan was so very brave," I said then, and it occurred to me that I might be slightly intoxicated. "He reminds me of you."

Was that the reason the visit to Stepney had affected me so?

Brodie looked up. "Is that so?"

I nodded as he pushed my hands aside and then unbuttoned my skirt and shirtwaist, then told me to stand.

I did, for the most part, with a hand on his shoulder to steady myself and stepped out of my clothes.

"I thought of Edinburgh and what it must have been like for you as a boy..."

He eased me down onto the bed, then tucked the bedcovers about me. I felt his hand against my cheek.

"Go to sleep, lass."

# Twelve

IT WAS late of the morning when I wakened. I sat up, a faint headache at the back of my head, as I remembered the evening before.

I rose, dressed then splashed water on my face from the basin. As I reached for the towel there was a vague memory of Brodie from the night before. However, the other side of the bed was undisturbed.

It appeared, as often happened, that he had been up most of the night. No doubt working on the case.

I attempted to put some order to my hair and caught my reflection in the mirror over the wash stand as I tied it back.

*"Are ye certain there isna a Scot in yer family somewhere with that red hair and that stubborn nature of yers?"* Brodie had once asked.

My family history through my great-aunt went back hundreds of years and innumerable ancestors. It was very possible there was a Scot in there somewhere, considering some of my ancestor's exploits and wanderings about.

It would serve him right of course, if there was.

The headache had subsided somewhat as I stepped out into the outer office.

Brodie was there, the earpiece of the telephone in hand, a frown on his face as I went to the coal stove. He had set the coffee pot to boil earlier and that wonderful aroma beckoned.

"*Aye*," he replied to the person on the other end of that call. There was nothing more and he hung up the earpiece somewhat abruptly.

I had gone to the blackboard, coffee mug in hand, and studied the notes I had made as well as the sequence of letters Lily had deciphered along with those numbers on that note that had been intercepted.

"Sir Avery," Brodie commented, the frown still there. "We are to report to him after ye've met with the curator at the museum."

A directive, which brought me back to the question— what were we dealing with? Something important that had everyone scurrying about most seriously. But what? And what was the connection to Dimitri Soropkin?

We knew when something was to happen— December eighteenth. Now, three days away. What was so important about that date?

"There are biscuits and ham that Miss Effie sent over this morning." He indicated the plate with a cloth over it on the desk.

"She seems to think that ye need a bit more flesh on yer bones."

My bones and the rest of me, along with the remnants of that headache, appreciated that very much.

"There were more, however the hound made off with several."

"And you still have all your fingers..." I remarked with some surprise as something tickled in the back of my brain, admittedly somewhat slow this morning.

"A narrow miss," he replied, then, "Wot is it?" he asked.

It was uncanny the way he had of sensing something I was thinking.

"A thought," I shook my head and then dismissed it. "You were out here all night?"

"Aye, going over yer notes," he gestured to the board. "And what ye learned about that message."

"Eighteenth of the month," I commented. "What is it about the eighteenth?"

"That is what we must find out. After we find out what the curator has to tell us about the doctor's notes."

He rose from the desk and rolled down the sleeves of his shirt. The view that I had been appreciating disappeared, hidden once more.

There was a somewhat critical look in my direction as I took a last bite of biscuit and gathered my bag.

"Ye might need some assistance with yer buttons so as not to give the curator the wrong impression when we arrive. And ye might need yer boots as well."

*The wrong impression.*

In consideration of Sir Reginald, who preferred ancient Egyptian ruins and most certainly was not the same sort as Brodie, I almost burst out laughing.

However, it did appear that I needed some assistance as I looked down. My shirtwaist was somewhat askew.

"Wot am I to do with a woman who canna even dress herself proper of a mornin'," he commented as he crossed the office to where I stood.

His warm fingers brushed my skin as he unbuttoned my

shirtwaist then realigned the buttons. I did have my own thoughts in the matter.

"I had not realized all the advantages," I commented as I watched those strong fingers and other thoughts arose.

"Advantages?" he replied as he finished straightening my clothes.

"To having a man about..." I explained.

That dark gaze narrowed as he seized my coat and held it for me.

"Other than the obvious reasons, of course," I added as I slipped through one arm, then the other, and smiled to myself at the softly muttered curse.

"Ye have no shame, woman."

"Very little," I replied. Most particularly, it seemed, when it came to Angus Brodie.

"This is most exciting!" Sir Reginald exclaimed after we arrived at the museum and found him in the Egyptian Hall— I did take a quick visual inventory to make certain that all the pieces on loan to my aunt had in fact been returned and now occupied their appropriate places.

"I spent most of the night going through the notes and the papyrus... magnificent, and such a find!" he went on almost beside himself.

His eyes closed much like someone enjoying a rare feast.

"You were able to make the translation?" I presumed.

"Oh my, yes." He was quite ecstatic. So much so, that I thought he might become apoplectic.

"As I suspected, the papyrus are written in Coptic. What a discovery! This will enhance our understanding of the

Egyptian culture. Imagine! Very near three thousand years old!"

"The translation, sir?" Brodie reminded him after I had made introductions.

"Of course. It's just that discoveries like this so far are rare. Actual written text! And to have a manuscript like this... Do come along and I will explain."

We followed him from the hall to his office.

It was much as I expected, having seen other such places in the museum. There were books lining the shelves, papers covering his desk, along with the manuscript I had asked him to translate, and...

Good heavens! A skull.

"This just arrived. I must often be both curator and archeologist."

Obviously, by his adoration of the skull, he preferred the latter.

"The skull was detached from the rest of the skeleton. Most unfortunate. However in proximity and in remarkable good condition in consideration of the amount of time that has passed. It was quite well preserved, except for being detached that is."

There was that, and I thought again of my preference for a Viking send off. Much simpler, and I wouldn't have someone poking about my bones sometime in the future.

"The person whom the skeleton belonged to appears to have been someone of some significance," he went on to explain about the discovery of the skeleton.

"There were ancient symbols etched into the stone covering his sarcophagus discovered at the temple at Edfu. Along with gold jewelry and a fascinating medallion, there were canopic jars that contained his heart and other organs.

I thought again of my preference, no jars for me with the thought that some *future* Mr. Brimley might have my heart in a container on his shelf.

"It seems that the mummification process, however, was either interrupted or perhaps never took place as the man is as you see him here."

Poor fellow, I thought.

Sir Reginald looked from Brodie to me, obviously expecting us to share his enthusiasm.

"Magnificent," I replied. Then I reminded him, "The papyrus found among Dr. Bennett's notes?"

"Oh, yes. Do forgive me, that is the reason you are here." He gestured to the chairs across from his desk, also covered in books and papers. He quickly gathered the papers, then circled round his desk and sat down. He adjusted his glasses.

"From other artifacts that have been found, it seems that the Egyptians were quite advanced in their medical treatments. With this, I was able to discern some very interesting procedures. See here," he carefully turned over a page of that ancient manuscript.

Brodie shook his head. "Cutting open a man's head to operate on his brain!" he exclaimed with obvious disgust and no small amount of doubt as our coach left the British Museum.

"They were quite advanced in a great many things—plumbing, water systems, astrology," I pointed out.

"There is plumbing in London," he pointed out. "And water systems built by the Romans, ye told me."

"How do you think they knew what to build?" I replied. "The Egyptians were far ahead of the Romans in that regard."

"The brain?" he made a disgusted sound.

It was not the procedures of the brain Sir Reginald had discovered in those ancient texts and then also in the doctor's notes, that caught my attention. And Brodie's as well.

"The complete restoration of a person's face."

"Fascinated with that, were ye?" Brodie commented.

"It seems that Dr. Bennett was as well." I thought of Ethan's injuries and the burns that were now healing.

"How remarkable, the ability to restore someone's features by using their own skin."

"Has anyone ever mentioned that ye have a somewhat odd fascination for such things?"

I had heard that before, present company included. I ignored it.

"You must admit that it seems that Dr. Bennett was able to use those same procedures to help Ethan," I pointed out as we reached Mayfair.

I wanted to change into something more appropriate for our meeting with Sir Avery.

"I believe that Mr. Brimley would call it an experiment," Brodie pointed out as we arrived and went to the front entrance where we were greeted by Mrs. Ryan and a most incredible aroma of food.

"However, as I have learned, inventions, procedures, everything begins with someone's experiment at some point in time."

"Ye have a peculiar nature, Mikaela. Most women would be taken with a new gown, a bit of furniture for the home, or a bouquet of flowers. However, ye are fascinated with surgeries of the brain and tissues."

"The doctor's notes referred to 'grafting' the skin at the site of the injuries," I corrected him as he moved in the direction of the dining room and kitchen.

"That is a remarkable aroma, Mrs. Ryan," he commented.

I headed for the stairs and my room to change.

"Making a statement, are ye, fer our meeting with Sir Avery?" Brodie commented as I returned.

I had chosen my gown with that in mind. Sir Avery did have a tendency of putting me in my place from time to time, as it were, or completely disregarding the points I had made in the past regarding a specific inquiry.

Brodie had intervened at the time, however, I had not forgotten those encounters. In addition he had sent Brodie off to Edinburgh with very little assistance that could have had disastrous consequences.

The Agency was important in the often delicate and frequently dangerous inquiries they made on behalf of the Crown. A somewhat murky organization to be certain.

I did, however, like Alex Sinclair very much, and trusted him. And it was obvious that Brodie was at least willing to use the Agency in matters that had proven difficult or almost impossible.

Case in point, that cryptic message that was intercepted and seemed very much connected to the death of Dr. Joseph Bennett.

"According to Templeton the color one wears conveys certain messages to anyone they encounter," I explained as the smell of Mrs. Ryan's roast chicken beckoned.

It had, after all, been some time since those biscuits and ham...

"And the source of her information?" Brodie asked as he pulled my chair out for me, then took the one at the opposite side of the table.

"She had it on good authority," I replied as Mrs. Ryan appeared with said chicken and set it on the table.

There were advantages to having her at the townhouse and I told her so.

"Someone has to prepare the food," this with a baleful look in my direction. "And with the two of you now, it makes it a pleasure. The saints know that you might starve with the lack of skill in the kitchen."

Brodie thanked her for her efforts and the fine meal as she returned to the kitchen.

"Good authority?" Brodie commented as he cut off a portion of the chicken for my plate then his.

I did hesitate on that, knowing what his reaction would be.

"A dead poet, perhaps?" he added.

William Shakespeare to be precise, whom Templeton claimed communicated with her on a regular basis, and with somewhat surprising accuracy in the past. It did make one consider the possibility.

"Playwright, not a poet," I clarified.

"And ye believe such things?"

"I believe in the *possibility* of such things," I replied.

The chicken was most delicious, quite different from my last efforts when I had abandoned undertaking such things in the future.

"It is not impossible," I continued. "According to Templeton, the afterlife is not at all what we have been led to believe."

"The man... spirit, whatever she thinks she hears... had some thoughts on that as well?"

I knew when I was being indulged, something along the line of— *"let her get it out, she'll be all right in a few moments."*

"Supposedly the soul returns into a new life, oftentimes somewhat similar to the previous one."

"Returns? From where?"

"From the spirit world," I gestured about, as if there was something stirring in the air about us.

"There are those who believe that is where the memory of things quite unexpected comes from, and other aspects."

"What other aspects?"

I did hesitate with this one, knowing him quite well with his somewhat cynical way of looking at things. However, there was always hope for enlightenment— with those experiments and surgical procedures that he had scoffed at in mind.

"There is every possibility that two souls may be destined to find one another."

"Such as Templeton finding Mr. Shakespeare? Munro should find that theory of yours most interesting."

There was a hint of amusement in reference to Templeton's past relationship with Munro. Actually, more than a hint. He was enjoying the conversation.

I didn't respond, but let him think on that, trusting that insightful intellect of his that I found so fascinating. For a man.

There it was, I thought, as his fork stopped midair and that dark gaze met mine.

"Ye're not suggesting... that you and I have met before in another life?"

"That could be most interesting," I suggested. "That fate or whatever you want to call it, crossed our paths once more."

He lowered his fork. "And wot might the circumstances of that previous life be?"

I had finished the meal and rose from the table. "According to Templeton, she might very well have been a man in that previous life and Munro..." I left the obvious unspoken.

"It's never quite certain how it will happen, you see. According to her *sources*..."

"And the color of yer gown?" Brodie asked as a coach arrived to take us to the Agency offices at the Tower of London for our scheduled meeting with Sir Avery.

"Purple? Although it is most becoming to ye."

He held my jacket then handed me my bag that contained notes I'd made during our meeting with Sir Reginald at the museum.

"Wot does it stand for according to Miss Templeton?"

We departed with my notes and a new urgency with the information we had learned, put off until the afternoon when Sir Avery apparently had time to meet with us.

"Power," I replied as Brodie gave the driver our destination.

# Thirteen

"YOU EXPECT me to believe that Soropkin may be out there somewhere with... as you called it, a new face, a different identity? Based upon what? Some ancient Egyptian text that Dr. Bennett was supposedly using. Ridiculous!"

Sir Avery rose from behind his desk, went to the door of his office, and closed it.

"That is the most ludicrous thing I have ever heard from you."

This directed at Brodie, which I found to be beyond irritating in consideration of the efforts he had made in the past on behalf of the Agency.

I summoned the "purple," as it were. Power. And then of course, there was the aspect of my red hair which Brodie was certain accounted for a great deal of my temperament.

"Nevertheless," I interjected. "It is noteworthy, and the Egyptian culture is far older than ours. According to Dr. Bennett's notes and the manuscript that clearly showed advanced procedures. It is very possible for someone's features to be changed through surgery. Possibly made to look quite different. And it is far more than you have been able to determine about Soropkin's whereabouts."

When he would have interrupted, no doubt to emphasize what he considered to be my lack of experience in such matters, I continued.

"You must admit that the evidence that we have brought you most certainly supports the possibility. And while you may consider it 'ridiculous,' I assure you there is a boy who is a living example of such a procedure. Therefore," I did take a breath.

"The question now, sir, is..." I was not devoid of common courtesies, even when addressing a pompous ass. And there were moments when they could be useful.

"Are you prepared to ignore the possibility at perhaps the cost of some cataclysmic event that Soropkin is well known for?"

To say that the following silence spoke volumes was another of those understatements.

"No, I am not. Well put, Lady Forsythe."

I prevented that moment of gloating over such an obvious victory.

"What then do you propose?"

I knew where this was leading from past meetings with Sir Avery. It was condescending in the least. He obviously hoped that having aired my feelings in the matter, that was the extent of it.

Not hardly.

"Mr. Brodie and I have some thoughts on that." And I deferred to him, more from concern that I might be quite blunt with a *proposal* for Sir Avery that had little to do with the inquiry case. Something more along the line of taking a leap in the river.

I did not say it as I have no difficulty knowing what is more important.

Over the next several hours, Brodie went over what we had learned by that return visit to Aldgate and with the translation of that Coptic text. For his part, Sir Avery sat and listened. I thought of old dogs and new tricks.

"What do you propose to do now?" Sir Avery asked, which included us both, at the conclusion of our meeting.

"There was a substance at the doctor's surgery in Aldgate" Brodie explained. "I know someone who may be able to tell us what that is. It could be important."

"And it is imperative that we determine what is to happen on the eighteenth of the month," I added. "That may very well tell us the reason Soropkin is here."

Sir Avery nodded. "If what you have presented here is true, then how do we find Soropkin once we have determined what is to happen on the eighteenth?"

That was very definitely the difficult part, I thought. If, in fact, Soropkin had his features changed by some surgical process performed by Dr. Bennett, he could be almost anywhere, and no one would know of it.

"We have three days," Brodie reminded him.

"This might be of some help," Sir Avery opened a file and pulled out a photograph. "Or perhaps not, if he has changed his appearance. We received this yesterday from Munich by courier." He handed the photograph to Brodie.

"It's not the best photograph and it was taken some time ago at the time of the Munich bombing that Soropkin claimed responsibility for. It was taken by one of those amateur photographers who happened to be at the rail station just before the explosion.

"According to our sources, the man under the clock in the

jacket with the collar turned up and cap, is Soropkin. We have been unable to find any other photographs. It's as if the man is a ghost."

Brodie handed it to me and tucked it into my bag.

"You're quite confident considering we're trying to find a *ghost*," I commented as we left the Tower.

I wanted to share that confidence, however, the task seemed most daunting.

"Perhaps some assistance from Templeton," he suggested as we reached High Street and found a cab where we parted.

He was off to see Mr. Brimley regarding that substance found at the doctor's office in Aldgate, while I was off to Mayfair to go back over everything we had learned so far.

There had to be something we were missing.

"It was good to see Mr. Brodie," Mrs. Ryan commented when I returned to the townhouse. "It's good to have a man to cook for," she added.

I could have sworn there was a muttered, "About time," in there somewhere.

"What was that, Mrs. Ryan?"

"I said there is mail, along with several of the dailies on your desk. And a note that was delivered this morning after you and Mr. Brodie left."

I investigated the mail first for any bills or other notices that needed payment, then found the envelope with that private note.

It was from Sir James. I opened the envelope and read the note inside.\

*There was no opportunity to speak at length the other evening.*
*Though it is somewhat short of notice, if you are not otherwise*
*engaged, perhaps you might join me for tea this afternoon,*
*or coffee that I remember you favored.*
*I am presently staying at the Grosvenor. No need to send round*
*a response.*
*If you cannot attend, I understand.*
*James Redstone*

Short notice to be certain, I thought. However, I was not one to be offended by it, particularly from an old friend. It would be good to see him again, and perhaps hear of his latest adventures.

I informed Mrs. Ryan that I would be going out.

"What should I tell Mr. Brodie, if he should return?" she asked.

"You may tell him that I'm meeting a friend for tea at the Grosvenor."

"There's the threat of weather." She frowned as she handed me my umbrella when the driver arrived.

I was quite familiar with the Grosvenor Hotel. My aunt frequently used it for her holiday events. It was convenient for guests traveling in from the countryside and offered accommodation if they chose to stay over.

I inquired at the concierge desk and was directed to the formal restaurant where I was told I would find Sir James.

There were several guests in the restaurant, including several officers of the military, quite resplendent in their uniforms.

The head waiter appeared. Sir James stood as I was escorted to his table.

"I was hoping you might join me." He then requested both tea and coffee.

When the waiter had gone, he added, "My compliments. You are very much the lady."

I removed my gloves. "I have been told that the color is bold."

He smiled. "Perhaps on another." Then, "It is quite exceptional to see you again, Mikaela. After our brief conversation, I thought that you might have taken offense at the topic in some way. However, I remembered your some-what passionate affinity for the downtrodden from our travels."

The waiter returned with both coffee and tea.

"A unique perspective among those of your station, that I understand you are still passionate about. I read with great interest your pursuits in Paris in the matter of the girl who was murdered in the box."

"With Mr. Brodie's assistance," I reminded him. "A most difficult inquiry," I added.

"An interesting pastime, but something that will be needed."

That seemed an odd response.

"It is somewhat more than a pastime," I replied, then suggested, "Tell me about your recent travels in Egypt."

He smiled. "It is unchanged as it has been for centuries."

Over coffee and tea we spoke of our mutual experience there, and his further travels there since.

As the hour passed, there was enthusiastic laughter among the officers the next table over. They did present a rather impressive sight, I thought, and I couldn't help but think of the young officer we had assisted previously and wondered where they might be bound.

Sir James seemed just as thoughtful as he watched them. "It is most sad."

"Sad?" I replied. That seemed such an odd thing to say.

"Men full of pride and honor," he made a sweeping gesture in their direction. "All to be wasted, sent off for Queen and Country by others who never know what it is to stand in the midst of battle, and for what? The power of the elite. The Empire? For the greed of others?"

He looked at me then. "Forgive me, my dear. I fear my travels have made me somewhat cynical. You will have more coffee perhaps?"

As he reached to pour the coffee, I saw his hand, those two fingers missing.

"A hunting accident?" I commented.

He looked at me with a bemused expression. "An unfortunate injury," he explained, then changed the conversation.

"You are now a married woman. Tell me of your husband. He seems quite a common chap. I understand that he is from the streets, a surprise when I first learned of it in consideration of your own family."

Brodie, a common chap? By whose measure, I thought, irritated by that.

"Not at all common," I replied. "We share many of the same interests. He is most resourceful, and kind," I added, a word I would not have thought of before. "He is most excellent at the things he cares about."

"And you admire that about him."

"Of course."

"Of course," he repeated with a thoughtful expression.

I chose to change the conversation.

"Where are you off to next?" I asked. "Or will you remain in London for a while?" I recalled that conversation I had overheard with Sir Robert about attending Parliament when next they met.

"I will be in London for a while. There are... matters to be seen to."

His father's estate I presumed, with his absence for several years.

"And you will be attending Parliament," I added.

"Yes, Sir Robert was kind enough to secure an invitation for me. The workings of the government are... most interesting."

The visit had been pleasant but I couldn't help but sense an undertone of some kind with those questions about Brodie and myself, his comments about the officers being sent off, as he put it, for the wealth and power of others.

I thanked him and stood to leave. He stood as well and took my hand.

"The world is changing, my dear. We will need those such as yourself and your husband for what is to come. There are those who rule the world, and those who choose to change it." He smiled then. "I do hope you are not offended by my thoughts."

"Not at all," I assured him, with the clear sense that this was not the man I had known from our travels; someone who was self-assured and as adventuresome as I was.

Sir James was not at all the man I remembered.

I returned to the townhouse. Brodie had called earlier and received my message.

It seemed that he was then off to follow information he had after his meeting with Mr. Brimley. And it further seemed that I was on my own for the evening and very possibly the entire night. Not that I didn't have something to occupy the time.

There was Dr. Bennett's book, the notes he had been compiling for his second book— his way of standing up against the Society of Medicine that he would sadly never be able to do now. There was the stack of daily newspapers from the last several days, and my own notes from our inquiry, including our meeting with Sir Reginald.

I let Mrs. Ryan know that there would be just one for supper.


I could have said that I had grown accustomed to working on my own, long evenings with Brodie off in one direction, myself off in another. In the past I had thought nothing of it, nor the evenings that often lengthened into the entire night...

Something had very definitely changed in that regard.

I realized that I very much liked his company, even when there was no conversation. The routine of an evening as he added coal to the fire at the office on the Strand, poured a cup of coffee or a dram of whisky for each of us, then listened as I rambled on about one thing or another, usually involving our latest case.

*"Add it to yer notes on the board..."* he would then say, when hardly more than two years before he would have grumbled that he couldn't make sense of my "scratchings" as he called them.

How was it that I had become accustomed to those grumblings, even looked forward to them? I smiled to myself.

According to my sister it was rare for a man to want to know what a woman was thinking, much less be concerned about it.

I knew from my own experience— that being the only version of marriage I believe existed and the reason I had previously avoided it —that she was right. It was simply that I had never thought I would encounter such.

I stared at the small medallion that I always wore, that gift from a man who valued my opinions, arguments, stubbornness, and realized that for the first time in my life, I missed someone. I missed Brodie.

Enough, I told myself, tucking the medallion back inside the neck of my gown. I had more than enough to do, and perhaps, just maybe I would find... something that would tell us what was to happen on the eighteenth of December.


Mrs. Ryan had long since bid me good night as the clock at the mantle struck one o'clock in the morning.

I stood from behind my desk. I had a headache from staring at the pages of Dr. Bennett's book, the notes he had made along with those from Sir Reginald, the daily newspapers, and that intercepted coded message.

I stretched, sorted through the notes and dailies one more time, then gave up and went upstairs to bed, and lay there, thoughts churning, that code and other bits and pieces of information nagging at me.

Somewhere after two of the morning the downstairs clock chimed and I drifted off.

I had discovered when writing my first novel, that the page is never finished, the light is never quite turned off, and sleep is merely a lie we tell ourselves as I sat upright in bed no more than three hours later. I threw back the covers and ignored the ice-cold floor as I raced downstairs, ignoring the fact that I might have fallen and broken my neck.

I turned on the electric in the small parlor that was my office and went to my desk. I sorted through everything I had been reading earlier— notes, papers, that coded message Lily had deciphered, that photograph Sir Avery had given us, then the dailies. One after the other tossed aside, like a mad woman, everything scattered about and covering the floor about the desk.

"It's here. I know it is. Bloody hell!"

"Saints preserve us, miss! What are you doin?" Mrs. Ryan, dragged from her own sleep by the noise I had made, or possibly my curses, stood in her nightshift and cap at the entrance to the parlor.

I waived the daily I was looking at her. "It's here. I knew that I had seen it!"

She stared at me as if I was that madwoman.

*1—8—1—2*

It was right in front of me all along. And now I was certain I had discovered more.

# Fourteen

I PUT a telephone call through to the office on the Strand, however there was no answer.

I frowned. It was then after six o'clock in the morning. It appeared that whatever Brodie had been pursuing, he had not yet returned.

At the more reasonable hour of eight o'clock, I had dressed, placed everything into my travel bag, and called for a driver.

On the ride to the office on the Strand, I kept thinking about my visit with Sir James, and the comments he had made about those in positions of power. For a man of his rumored wealth that seemed unusual. And then there had been his comment about Brodie— a *common man* as he had called him.

In consideration of the early hour, before the usual daily traffic on the street set in, I arrived at the office in good time.

I paid the driver then crossed the Strand to the sidewalk below the office. When I would have gone to the stairs, Mr. Cavendish appeared quite suddenly in front of me and blocked my path.

"Is Mr. Brodie in?" I asked.

"He came back a while ago. Wait, miss!"

I was more than a little surprised as he tried to stop me.

"Thank you," I replied and stepped around him.

There was immediately the sound of the bell that rang furiously at the top landing, used to announce an arrival. I did wonder what that was about as I gathered my skirt and ran up the stairs.

I was met by Brodie, as he stepped out of the office and blocked my going any further. However, not before I caught a glimpse inside.

A man was seated on a chair in the middle of the room and Mr. Conner was standing over him. The man in the chair was quite bruised and bloodied.

*"Now, let's start over,"* I heard Mr. Conner say. *"And ye will give me the information I want this time..."*

Then Brodie closed the door.

"What is that about?" I asked.

Brodie's response was to seize me by the arm and turn me back toward the stairs. The expression on his face was like stone.

"The man has information that may be useful regarding Soropkin," he replied.

The method of questioning him seemed a bit extreme, perhaps even brutal, I thought.

"I have some information as well. I'm certain that I have found the event for the eighteenth December indicated in that message..."

"Aye." He proceeded to escort me back down the stairs.

"I thought you might want to know..." Once more I was cut off.

"It could be important," I did manage to say as I attempted to free my arm.

"I understand."

I hardly thought so.

"I need you to go to the Public House and wait there," he then told me.

"What is it?" I demanded. "What has happened?"

"I will explain when I meet ye there." And for emphasis he added, "I'll not argue the matter with ye, Mikaela."

I was not accustomed to this from him. If it was anyone else, I would have simply told them to stuff it as my friend Templeton was known to say, and then would have done as I pleased.

However...

"I'll be waiting," I frostily replied. I could always tell him to "stuff it" later.

I ordered coffee at the Public House and waited.

It was very near a full hour before Brodie finally appeared. I had seriously considered leaving, but there was that nagging little voice inside my head. I was curious about that scene at the office.

Miss Effie brought a second cup and fresh coffee.

"Mornin', Mr. Brodie," she greeted him. "Out and about early?"

He nodded and thanked her, then looked across the table at me.

"Before ye get yer temper up, there are reasons I sent ye away."

"Before?" I pointedly replied.

He ignored that. "It was not the place for ye to be at the time."

When I would have said something more, he shook his head.

There was something in his manner and the expression on his face. He obviously had little sleep the night before. That little voice cautioned that I at least listen to what he had to say.

"I had word from Sir Avery regarding additional information they received by way of telegram after we met with him," he began, stopped, then continued.

"It seems that yer friend, Sir James Redstone, is very probably involved in the situation."

"Ridiculous!" I replied quite vehemently which drew the attention of others about us.

I then asked with lowered voice. "Based upon what evidence?"

I should have known better. Brodie did not make assumptions or make statements without evidence to back it up. Still, there was a certain attitude ever since he had met Sir James.

Jealousy perhaps? The word was there, but that was hardly something that fit the man that I knew. With other things Brodie was prone to— stubbornness, a strong will, and that bloody Scot temper —jealousy didn't make the list.

"There are those who saw him in Munich as recently as six weeks ago, contrary to the fact that he would have everyone believe that he just returned from Egypt."

I wanted to tell him that it wasn't unusual to have a stop-over after being abroad for an extended period of time. I had done so with a short stay in Paris after returning from Budapest — a visit with an acquaintance of my aunt.

However, there was more.

"The man Mr. Conner was questioning is a middleman. He connects certain people, for a price. He arrived from Munich six weeks ago and secured a substantial space at a warehouse that yer friend at the gymnasium in German Town learned of, to store a large shipment he was expecting. And it seems that Sir James made inquiries at the warehouse."

He referred to Herr Schmidt, a friend who had provided information in the past. And six weeks ago, once more. That seemed to be a common aspect, as far as it went.

"The shipment contained several explosive munitions and weapons."

I knew from previous investigations that such shipments had been discovered in the past.

"There's more." He hesitated. "Mr. Brimley has determined the substance found at Dr. Bennett's private surgery in Aldgate. It was a form of opium."

Perhaps not unusual, I thought. A physician's surgery, bottles of other medicines and tonics, a preventative for pain such as that for young Ethan.

"The residue was somewhat thick from the substance that contained the opium," he went on to explain. "I had noticed something else and had Mr. Brimley return afterward and investigate."

"And?" I asked the obvious question.

"It was a fingerprint."

Again, not surprising in and of itself.

He took a long drink of coffee, thoughtful, then set the cup down.

"Perhaps a valuable piece of information," I commented. "If it can be matched to someone..."

Although we both knew that the results of such things could be disappointing as there was only the most rudimentary of records with the MET. Perhaps the Agency had additional information.

"It matched the print that Mr. Brimley was able to take

from Sir James' cup at the Grosvenor after ye met with him."

I couldn't say anything for a moment. Then, "You had me followed? Of all the...!"

"There's more ye should know," he continued. "Redstone was not a guest of the hotel. It appears that he's been staying some other place, some place he didna want others to know about."

"His family home is in London," I informed him. "He has returned to settle the estate. You are not well informed."

I stood abruptly as several other things then came to mind. Telling him to "stuff it" seemed mild by comparison.

He stood as well and reached out, his hand closing around my wrist when I would have simply left him there.

"Ye're smarter than to be angry about this! Think what I've told ye and remember that people are dead because of what is goin' to happen, including Dr. Bennett! And perhaps a good many more if we canna stop this."

Never let it be said that I didn't see what he was talking about, startling as it was. And yet the thought that Sir James was part of something like this... Still...

It wasn't as if I hadn't sensed things and then simply dismissed them. I slowly sat back down.

"You could have told me you were having him followed."

"There was no time, and ye seemed quite taken with the man."

"How did you know that I was meeting Redstone at the Grosvenor?" I then asked, but the answer was there— "Mrs. Ryan."

"Ye told her yerself that ye were going to the Grosvenor. It seems that ye left in a hurry. She found the note on the floor that he sent ye."

And just happened to see his name, I thought.

"It was out of concern for ye when I telephoned the town-house. Right or wrong, ye mean a great deal to her after the loss of her daughter. I'll not have ye put any blame on her for it."

He was right, of course. Mrs. Ryan was more than my housekeeper, particularly after the loss of Mary in that first inquiry case that also included my sister's disappearance.

Stunning as it was, the evidence was there. Still, I was not over the fact that he had kept it from me.

"What is to be done?" I asked.

"Ye did say that ye have figured out the meaning of those numbers."

I nodded. "The eighteenth day of the twelfth month—December," I replied. "Something is to happen tomorrow, and then I read the announcement in the dailies that the Queen is to dedicate the new war memorial."

"Aye, that supports what we suspected. If Soropkin is part of this, it makes even more sense given past incidents that he's instigated."

It was an attempt, I knew, to ease the tension between us. Like tossing a bone to a dog?

However, not quite enough.

"Has Soropkin been found?"

"No, and that is the worry. He is still out there as well. The man seems to have an uncanny ability to blend in and then disappear."

He assured me that he would contact Sir Avery with the information about a potential target for Soropkin, and possibly bolstering what they already suspected.

He paid for the coffee then escorted me from the Public House.

It seemed that Mr. Conner had concluded his "question-ing" of the man I had glimpsed at the office.

"He was well paid, more than I earned even after twenty years with the Met," he commented, as I looked about for some sight of the man, or perhaps a body?

Mr. Conner did seem quite pleased with himself in spite of a bruised fist.

"A thousand pounds paid to him... by Sir James Redstone."

In consideration of what Brodie had told me, it was hardly surprising.

"Wot else was he able to tell ye?" Brodie asked.

"It seems that the job he was paid for has to do with the Queen's dedication of the war memorial tomorrow."

Brodie nodded with a look at me. "Aye, what else?"

"The payment was for the man and his people to arrange to have a barrier in place at a specific location along the route the Queen will be traveling from Buckingham Palace."

A barrier, and then an attack on the Queen? As there had been attacks on members of the ruling monarchs in two other countries?

"I might argue the politics of it," Mr. Conner added. "I still believe that Scotland should be our own country. However, I canna condone the murder of an old woman."

He referred to the fact that Britain was now governed by a constitutional monarchy. The Queen was now more or less a figurehead rather than the ruler of the country, who made suggestions and recommendations to Parliament rather than setting out laws herself with the assistance of her council as in the past.

"Ye have the location the man told ye?" Brodie asked.

Mr. Conner nodded. "I telephoned the Agency and gave the information to Sir Avery's people. They'll see that protections are put in place."

"What about Soropkin?" I asked.

Mr. Conner shook his head. "The man claimed that he only met with Redstone. According to what he told me, he knew nothing about Soropkin." He rubbed his bruised knuckles.

"I believe that he was telling the truth."

"And Redstone?" Brodie asked.

Mr. Conner shook his head. "There's been no word."

Was it possible that Sir James was part of all of this? I thought of everything over the past few days since his return, and things he had said. I had simply brushed it aside. And what of the injury to his hand, that had obviously happened since our travels together? An accident, he had called it. But what sort of accident?

I stood before the blackboard in the office. I still found it difficult to believe that Sir James was involved in a threat against the Queen. It did not seem like the man I had met years before.

He was from a well-titled family. If he was involved in this, it was against everything he'd been born to. Still, as I thought back to the day before at the Grosvenor, the things he said, and his comments about the Queen. There were indications that I had dismissed at the time as nothing more than the usual conversations one might hear at a social gathering or event. Or perhaps chose to ignore.

I thought of Mr. Conner's comment about Scotland, not an uncommon sentiment, particularly among the Scots.

Was it possible that with changes Scotland might one day be independent? And what would that mean?

I had added more notes from the information Mr. Conner and Brodie had obtained.

Buckingham Palace was notified as well. Sir Avery was informed that the Queen was adamant, however, in that stalwart manner that people had come to admire about her. *"Getting on with it,"* as she had been quoted in the past through her own difficulties and losses.

Brodie had also made arrangements to be present the next day where that barrier was to have been placed, along with Mr. Conner and a substantially increased number of the Metropolitan Police, Sir Avery's people, and the Royal Guard.

Hours passed, though it seemed like days, since I had arrived earlier that morning. I caught the scent of food that Mr. Cavendish had undoubtedly brought over from the Public House. However, I had no appetite.

Mr. Conner had left earlier with arrangements made to meet Brodie the next morning. There had been messages delivered by Alex from the Agency as other arrangements were confirmed.

However, there had been no further conversation between Brodie and myself.

I was admittedly hurt, as if he didn't trust that I would see the truth of the information he and Mr. Conner had obtained. Then I had been deliberately excluded from something that involved both the inquiry case about Dr. Bennett's murder and the investigation that Brodie was pursuing.

In the past, there had been a partnership between us, the sharing of information, of speculation and thoughts with the notes that I made at the bloody damned blackboard!

Yet today, I had been shut out from the latest information with that comment that I seemed *"quite taken with Sir James."* Did he believe that I could not be trusted with the information?

That was perhaps what hurt the most, particularly in consideration of our personal relationship.

After Mr. Conner left, Brodie had encouraged me to make my notes on the board with the new information we now had. However, it seemed gratuitous. Much like a pat on the head for a faithful hound.

"Ye're still angry," Brodie said in a quiet voice.

That didn't begin to describe it, I thought, but didn't say it. I didn't say anything at all but continued to make my notes, as if I had not heard him.

There was something more in all of this, something I was convinced that I would find in my notes if I stared at them long enough— my scratchings on the board as Brodie called them.

Or perhaps it was merely a way to ignore him. Although Angus Brodie was hard to ignore.

"I understand."

The piece of chalk snapped against the board, and my anger with it. I turned on him.

"Do you?" I replied, then vented the anger.

"I thought we had a partnership that included trust, respect, consideration of each other's ideas, and..." There was that other part, of course. "You set it all aside as if none of that mattered."

"Dinnae do this, Mikaela. Now, is not the time."

I ignored the warning. It most certainly was the time.

"Is it all a lie, then?" I continued. "Our work together? It certainly wasn't on my part. Or was it ambition?

"Perhaps something Sir Avery promised you that got in the way even though you don't trust the man?" I added.

"No."

To which question? I thought.

"Then, what the bloody hell is it?" I demanded.

"This is not the proper time with Soropkin still out there. There are too many things at stake."

There most certainly were.

"Proper time?" I replied and made no attempt to disguise the anger. Of all the absurd things he could have said.

"Aye, proper, between the two of us."

"Exactly," I replied. "However, you chose..."

He cut off what I was about to say.

"It was about ye."

That set me back, but only momentarily.

"If this is about protecting me, we've already had that conversation."

Numerous times, as a matter of fact. He rounded the desk and came toward me— or perhaps stalked was a better word.

I refused to be intimidated.

"And you will not use that excuse." I informed him at the same time I considered blackening his other eye.

"Aye, ye have proven that... and I accept it as far as it goes."

Whatever that was supposed to mean.

"However, with what we have now learned, I thought that if ye still had feelin's for the man..."

I stared at him— feelings for Redstone?

There were several things I could have said. I didn't. Instead I pushed my way past him and went to the desk.

I shoved Dr. Bennett's book into my bag, along with the notes he had made for his second book, and those ancient papyrus notes.

"Mikaela...!"

"Yes, of course," I replied with a full measure of cynicism. "That explains everything."

I went to the door, then down the stairs to the street below. Brodie didn't follow, and I was grateful for that. I didn't want him to follow me. At that moment I didn't want to see him.

I didn't wait for Mr. Cavendish to find a driver, but instead crossed the Strand at a furious pace, then continued down the opposite side to the cross street and waved down a driver.

The townhouse was quiet when I returned.

Mrs. Ryan made a brief appearance. She took one look at me and frowned.

"You've spoken with Mr. Brodie?"

I did not answer, which I suppose was an answer in itself.

She made a sound, one that I would have sworn was very like Brodie's.

"Give me my notice then if you intend to do so, but I'll not apologize," she announced, then returned to the kitchen.

I had no intention of doing so, of course. Brodie was right, at least in that. However, he was still a horse's ass, and I would have told him to his face if he was there.

# Fifteen

AFTER MAKING my feelings known the previous afternoon, I usually would have slept quite soundly, particularly with very few hours sleep the night before.

I didn't. And like the night before, I rose somewhere near four in the morning and returned to my desk in the front parlor.

I spread out everything that I had gathered regarding Dr. Bennett's murder and Brodie's investigation into Soropkin. Along with that cryptic message that had been intercepted and seemed to confirm what was planned by Soropkin.

I then read the notes Dr. Bennett had made for that second book that he would now never write. He had been fascinated with the possibilities of restorative surgery that included of all things... the possibility of full restoration of one's facial features.

It certainly seemed that he had been able to provide that for Ethan. However, between his notes and those ancient procedures written almost three thousand years earlier in those papyrus texts that Sir Reginald had been able to translate for me, I had discovered far more.

The ability to restore someone's features seemed almost too incredible to believe, yet according to those ancient procedures it seemed more than possible with descriptions of specific surgeries that had been performed and documented. What other possibilities might come from that?

Soropkin came to mind. He had been seen weeks earlier in London and followed to Aldgate where Dr. Bennett had set up that secret office. He had then disappeared, vanished, and Brodie, along with the resources of the Agency, had been unable to find him.

Was it possible that he had gone to Dr. Bennett for just such a surgery? The implications were horrifying, and yet... If I allowed myself to take that next step, past the impossible and the horror of it, the possibility was there.

With a different face, how easy might it be to move about without anyone the wiser?

*"Bulldog with a bone"* Brodie had said of me more than once.

I knew where it came from, the need to have order, to understand everything, to know the most minute detail, then examine it, find the reason— when everything seemed to spin out of control.

I thought of my father. Like it or not, the man had affected both my sister and I with his presence, and lack of; his lies and deceptions, and then the manner in which he ended his life. I had struggled with it most of my life it seemed, hating him for what he'd done. Then attempting to run away from it all as my great-aunt once suggested.

*"What is... simply is,"* she told me after one of my episodes as she called them with great wisdom, when I had taken myself

off into the forest at Old Lodge and not returned until the following day, in spite of her gamesman's warning that there were dangers there.

*"You must accept what has happened, move on, and not waste time on someone that doesn't matter."*

That seemed so very simple at the time but hardly a salve for my anger at our father. There was more, she told us, as there usually was when Linnie or I seemed to be having a rough go of it.

*"Ask yourself, can you change the sort of man your father was?"* she asked me at the time, and had then proceeded to answer the question herself.

*"No, you cannot! You might wish to drag the man out of his coffin and kick him in the shins, or worse. But be done with it, child. Trust me, there are good men. I promise you."*

It had taken me a while to absorb that. After all, I was only ten years old at the time. But I knew that she was right.

Brodie was a good man. I had known it from the beginning, even if it had taken me a while to acknowledge it.

Perhaps that was the reason the conversation the day before had infuriated me so... that he thought that I might *"still have feelings for Sir James?"*

Feelings that I knew were nothing more than admiration for someone who had traveled widely, was far more experienced and worldly than myself, and for those several weeks that we traveled together had indulged someone who quite simply, was not experienced or worldly.

It hurt that Brodie seemed to think so little of me.

If I hadn't been so angry at the time, I would have heard what wasn't said. There was almost a sadness in his voice, as I thought back on it. Perhaps fear that he might be right? It seemed that I had unknowingly hurt him as well.

The mantle clock chimed— half past eight o'clock, a reminder that the Queen's procession and dedication of the memorial was scheduled for two hours from now.

I knew from past events that people would already be gathering along the procession route the Queen was to take from Buckingham Palace to the memorial.

I could not stay here and simply wait to receive word of whatever might or might not happen.

I had already checked to make certain the revolver in my bag was loaded, then called for Mrs. Ryan as I went to the stairs to dress.

"Yes, miss?" she said, quite formal as she arrived from the kitchen where I had heard her earlier slamming a pot, then a dish, in somewhat of a pique it seemed.

"I will need a driver."

"Yes, miss...?" she said hesitant.

"Is that some of your wonderful coffee, I smell?"

"Most certainly, miss," she replied, the hesitance in her voice gone.

I dressed and had finished my second cup of coffee along with some of Mrs. Ryan's spectacular sponge cake— Rupert would have been jealous —by the time the driver arrived.

It had been a somewhat longer wait than usual, he apologized, as there were delays due to detours and road closures in preparation for the Queen's appearance for the dedication.

The park where the ceremony was to take place was not far from Buckingham Palace with Parliament a few blocks beyond — near the river.

The traffic on the street was abominable the nearer the driver approached the park. He was forced to take the long way around, then approached from Whitehall Road which was hardly better.

There were other coaches and carriages, along with those who chose to walk to the park that included properly dressed ladies and gentlemen, as well children and more than one pram, along with dozens of officers of the MET both afoot and astride.

From what Brodie had shared with me the day before, there were undoubtedly Sir Avery's people scattered among the crowd as well as the Royal Guard.

And somewhere among them were Brodie, Mr. Conner, and undoubtedly Munro. It did seem that every possible precaution had been taken.

The coach rolled to a stop once more and the driver called down.

"Sorry, miss. The way through is blocked."

I departed the coach then continued afoot toward the park, along with what seemed the entire population of London.

I eventually made it to the edge of the green, more or less pushed along by the crowd that always gathered when the Queen or any member of the royal family was out and about.

I managed to extricate myself from the crowd as they surged forward and found a place at the curb along the thoroughfare just across the way from the memorial.

As the crowd gathered, joined by more people, I eventually heard the expectant buzz of conversation from the crowd around me as the Queen's coach came into view down the thoroughfare.

Rather than the gold coach used for her coronation and other state events, she had chosen the simple black coach she seemed to prefer since the death of Prince Albert years before.

The Royal Guard led the way with more mounted guards that followed.

As her coach drew closer, I searched the crowd nearby for any indication of an attack— any sudden movement, someone abruptly pushed out of the way as someone else attempted to get closer, or the sudden sound of alarm from the crowd. However, everything seemed quite calm.

There was nothing out of the ordinary as the Queen's coach rolled past then stopped in front of the memorial. Nor when she stepped down and was then escorted toward the memorial to make the dedication.

The ceremony was quite somber and brief, and soon ended as the Dean of Westminster Abbey provided the blessing.

The Queen remained for a time, exchanging conversation with him, then she was escorted back to her coach, a solitary figure in perpetual black mourning, the Royal Guard at attention with stoic expressions.

I scanned the crowd again, but there was nothing that indicated an attack or disturbance, no sudden sharp noises or someone running forward as the royal coach slowly circled back around the way it had come then departed for the return to Buckingham Palace.

Was it possible those involved had learned that Sir Avery's people were aware of their plans? Or was that information false?

Brodie had described Soropkin as methodical, perhaps even a genius, and completely dedicated to his cause. He was undoubtedly quite mad and extremely dangerous.

It obviously didn't matter that his plans to strike against all authority already had resulted in hundreds of senseless deaths and would inevitably result in millions more should all of Europe be thrown into chaos and eventually... all out war.

History would once again repeat itself and innocent men, women, and children would pay the ultimate price for that madness.

No, I thought. From what I had heard about Soropkin, he wouldn't merely set aside his plans if it was revealed that the authorities had discovered them. There had to be more, something we were missing.

As the crowd began to disperse, I watched others near the memorial searching for sight of either Brodie or Mr. Conner.

Many of those who had watched the ceremony, including what appeared to be several members of Parliament in their frock coats, returned now to Westminster Palace, that sprawling Gothic center of English government. So-called as it had once been the residence of the king, several hundred years past, and now where the houses of Parliament met.

It was then I saw Sir James. He was standing very near the memorial. As I watched, he turned and set off at a brisk pace toward the Palace.

Was he there merely to attend the session as it reconvened after the ceremony, with that invitation that Sir Robert Crosswhite was to have provided? Or was there something else at work?

Brodie had insisted that Sir James might very well be involved in Soropkin's plot. Impossible as that seemed and as much as I didn't want to believe it, it was possible and the urgency with which he crossed the green, then the street that ran before that sandstone behemoth of English history, suggested otherwise.

I thought again of what we knew:

Soropkin, a known anarchist and extremely dangerous, had been seen in London weeks before, and had then disappeared;

Dr. Bennett had been murdered in that secret office in

Aldgate where he had performed procedures censured by the Society of Medicine;

Sir James had returned. Not from an extended travel of several months to Egypt and the Far East that he would have everyone believe, but more recently from Munich that Brodie had learned through communications received by the Agency. And further proof that he was in Munich at the time of the attack there;

Then, that cryptic message that had been intercepted in Luxembourg.

*"Everything is in place"*... and the date I had finally unscrambled— along with the eighteenth of December. Today's date.

There was more that I had not known until the day before.

The deception of our meeting for afternoon tea at the Grosvenor, where Sir James was not a guest after all as he had led me to believe, and our conversation, his comments about my abilities and my position as a member of a titled family.

While his compliments seemed like flattery at the time, I hadn't been impressed. As Brodie had pointed out in our conversation the day before, it did seem as if there might have been another motive.

It was very possible, he had insisted, that it was an attempt to persuade me to become part of some cause.

And then there was the part of the message that had so far eluded us:

*P A R and L S*

The more I thought of it, standing there at the edge of the green, the facts and clues were undeniable. I thought again of that last part of that message... then turned and looked for Brodie or Mr. Conner again.

Why had I not seen it? PAR for Parliament, not PARLS, that had confused me. And then LS.

Or perhaps I chose not to see it because of that old friendship.

The sound of my name pulled me from my thoughts and that stunning certainty as Mr. Conner and Alex Sinclair approached. I ran toward them.

"The target is not the Queen! It never was." I glanced back in the direction I had seen Sir James as he disappeared through the crowd.

"The target is Parliament and the Prime Minister! It was in those last letters in that intercepted message. And Redstone is here!"

"Dear God," Alex replied. "Are you certain about the message?"

I repeated the letters. "The target is Parliament— PAR, and the last two letters LS..."

"The Prime Minister, Lord Salisbury," Alex replied.

"Where did you see him?" Mr. Conner demanded.

"At the entrance."

"Then, he's already inside."

"Where's Brodie?" I asked.

"With Sir Avery and his men." Mr. Conner's expression was grim. "I'll find him."

By the time they learned that Redstone was there and what I was now certain of, it might be too late. And Soropkin? Was he somewhere inside Parliament even now?

"We have to stop him," I replied, and turned toward that massive hall that sat at the bank of the Thames.

"Foolish woman! Ye'll not go alone," Mr. Conner shouted

after me, then, "go with her, lad! And don't let her out of yer sight, or we'll both answer to Mr. Brodie for it."

I didn't wait for Alex as I pushed my way through the crowd and followed the direction Redstone had gone.

He caught up with me at the main entrance to Westminster Hall as the returning members— hundreds of them, along with staff and guests, were forced to queue into a single crowded line at the clerk's desk at the entrance.

Alex looked about and then at me with new urgency.

"However will we ever find him?"

I had the same thought with the line before us. If Redstone had managed to gain entrance, we might not find him until it was too late.

The whole of Parliament was massive and filled the embankment at the river, a maze of what had once been a royal residence along with apartments for visiting dignitaries and members, and offices, committee rooms connected by lobbies and passages on multiple floors.

It all converged at the Central Hall that eventually connected to the House of Commons and House of Lords with private offices for members of Parliament that numbered in the hundreds.

To find anyone it was required to set an appointment, and then still be forced to wait for hours or return another time if Parliament was in an extended session as today with the dedication at the park.

Not finding Redstone was not an option.

There were the usual conversations among those who waited to sign back in, complaints about the delay and the late hour members would all be there, along with a conversation between two members.

"It will be even later into the evening," one of them commented, "with the P.M. to address the Commons."

Alex and I exchanged a glance. The Prime Minister, Lord Salisbury, was to speak at the House of Commons. We both knew the meaning of that, a perfect opportunity for anyone with a plan to attack Parliament and Lord Salisbury.

Alex nodded. "We have no time for this delay."

He reached inside his coat and I glimpsed the note he reached for, along with something most unusual. He was carrying a revolver!

He pulled out the note, then cut his way through the line ahead, with complaints and grumblings from those around him. I took advantage of his cut through the queue and followed him.

He ignored the complaints as he reached the clerk's desk.

"Where would Lord Salisbury be at this time?" he demanded.

Startled, the clerk was taken aback.

"I beg your pardon, sir. You must wait your turn."

"There is no time." Alex thrust the note at him. "We are here on behalf of Sir Avery Stanton and the office of Special Services."

In spite of the urgency, Alex kept his voice low.

"There has been a threat, and I suggest you make every accommodation." He again demanded, "Where is Lord Salisbury at this time? Unless of course, you wish to be arrested."

I would not have guessed that Alex Sinclair, with his codes and machines and that unruly mop of hair he was forever pushing back from his glasses could be so assertive.

And as for that note he had shown the clerk, I had caught a brief glimpse of an emblem at the top of the note, along with Sir Avery's signature at the bottom. It was a royal warrant.

"Not at all, sir," the clerk hastily replied and handed the note back to Alex. "That is, yes, of course. The Prime Minister would most usually be in a private office next to the members retiring room, preparing for his address before the members."

"I need to speak with the Home Secretary immediately," Alex insisted. "And we will need someone to take us to that office."

"The Home Secretary is presently scheduled to meet in the House of Commons," the clerk informed us.

"I don't care if he's meeting with the Queen," Alex replied. "You're to send for him now! Or there may well be no Parliament. Is that clear?"

We were asked to stand apart as I wondered where Redstone was and what had been planned.

Eventually Secretary Mathews, the Home Secretary, appeared, quite agitated.

"What is the meaning of this?" he demanded.

Alex pulled him aside and quickly explained the reason we were there. Secretary Mathews looked up with a tight expression.

"I know Sir Avery quite well," he said. Then asked, "Where did you last see Redstone?"

"Crossing the green and then at the entrance," I replied. "He disappeared inside. And there is a man that is also part of this— Dimitri Soropkin."

By the expression on his face, he obviously knew of Soropkin. He immediately went and questioned the clerk, then returned.

"There is no note of Redstone's arrival. If, as you say, he managed to get past the desk, he could be anywhere." The Home Secretary looked at Alex.

"You're certain about the threat?"

"Most certain," he replied.

I explained how Sir James might have been able to gain entrance without being questioned or required to sign in.

"He's to be the guest of Sir Robert Crosswhite by special invitation."

The enormity of the threat was not lost on the Home Secretary. He motioned to the officer who had accompanied him.

"You are to take Mr. Sinclair and Miss Forsythe to the office presently occupied by the Prime Minister and remain there. Go quickly and as quietly as possible," he added. "We need to clear everyone from the building, and I don't want people in a panic situation. Is that understood?"

He intended to clear as many people as possible from Parliament. A daunting task to be certain. And the amount of time that would take? Surely Redstone and Soropkin would take notice. What then?

Alex took me by the arm, and we followed our escort down the Commons hallway to the offices in the adjacent passageway where there were more offices along with that private office that had been set apart for Lord Salisbury.

The officer knocked at the door then opened it. "There is a situation, sir," he announced as we entered the office.

"The Home Secretary has asked that you remain here. These people will explain."

"We've uncovered a situation, sir, that could be extremely dangerous," Alex then went on to tell the Prime Minister.

"There is the possibility of an attack against you as well as the members of Parliament. Precautions are being taken," he continued.

I saw the faint twitch at the corner of Lord Salisbury's eyes, the way the light from the overhead chandelier gleamed almost unnaturally on his forehead and cheeks above his side whiskers.

There was something different about the man I had encountered briefly in the past at a handful of society functions that I was unable to avoid with one excuse or another.

"I see," Salisbury curtly replied with amazing calm, then a glance at the uniformed officer who had accompanied us.

"I must leave," he suddenly announced, and headed for the door.

"Sir! I must protest! It could be extremely dangerous..." Alex moved to stop him with a hand on his arm.

As the Prime Minister reached the door, the sleeve of his coat pulled back ever so slightly at his wrist.

He immediately pulled it back into place and would have insisted on opening the door. Alex stopped him.

The Prime Minister's gaze abruptly met mine. He knew what I had seen.

There was a mark on his wrist, a tattoo. A very distinct tattoo!

I was no stranger to them. Point of fact, I had one of my own, acquired on one of my travels. But this one had specific significance.

It was a tattoo of a black hand, the anarchist's symbol that I had seen on that banner in Budapest, a tattoo that Soropkin supposedly also had as well as those loyal to him!

"Get out of my way!" Salisbury demanded.

"Sir, you must remain here!" Alex repeated.

The blow caught Alex by surprise. It was a glancing blow to the face, momentarily surprising him.

"Stop him!" I told the officer who had accompanied us. "He's not the Prime Minister, he's an impostor!" And a very dangerous one.

The officer was slow to react, or possibly didn't believe what I was saying. Lord Salisbury, or the man who wanted us to believe he was Salisbury, would have bolted out the door if I hadn't caught him by the back of his coat.

I had the advantage of height. He had the advantage of greater weight as he turned with a revolver in his hand.

I struck it away, landed the blow to his left cheek, then swept his feet out from under him.

He landed hard, then scrambled to retriever the revolver. However, I was able to reach it first.

The "Prime Minister" pushed to his feet on a flood of curses and would have escaped if Alex hadn't grabbed him by the front of his coat.

He glared back at me through the swollen eye above his cheek that bled profusely.

I stared at the damage, not the same sort as the blow I had given Brodie, barely a bruise that had already faded.

This was different and quite ghastly as blood seeped from a hair-thin scar that had barely healed and had ruptured open, a flap of skin sagging away from his cheek. Grafted skin peeling away.

Mr. Brimley had spoken of the possibility of such a surgery during our visit with young Ethan after reading Dr. Bennett's notes, and that ancient Coptic text that Sir Reginald had translated. Procedures over three thousand years old practiced by the Egyptians that Dr. Bennett had lectured on and was then censured for. A new face in place of the old one.

In Ethan's case to restore a young boy's features after he had been horribly burned.

What was I staring at now? An entirely new face to hide one's identity?

"Good heavens!" Alex said, equally stunned. "You needn't

have struck so hard."

"I didn't," I assured him, then introduced him.

"Meet Dimitri Soropkin."

Alex looked at me as if I might have taken several steps away from sanity.

"You don't mean..."

"At the inside of his right wrist you will find a tattoo of a black hand. It is the mark of the anarchist and those who follow him."

"Hold him!" Alex ordered the officer. "Do not let him escape."

"He said that you were quite extraordinary," the man I was now certain was Soropkin said in a scathing tone.

"A woman!" he spat out as the officer produced manacles and snapped them shut about his wrists.

"Intelligent, fearless, someone who understood the injustices that are all around us. He believed that he could persuade you to join us."

By that, I assumed that he meant Redstone.

His English was almost perfect, just as that face that Dr. Bennett had given him was almost perfect. But not quite.

"He was wrong. You see, I remember Kosta Resnick." The man who had led the assassination attempt against the Prince of Wales in that first inquiry case with Brodie.

"And Marie Nicola who was responsible for killing an innocent young woman," I added, the memory still painful. Mary Ryan, my housekeeper's daughter who was brutally murdered, and my sister might very well have been their next victim.

"So, you see, it was never possible to persuade me."

"Where is the Prime Minister?" Alex demanded.

Soropkin smiled, a gruesome expression given his now

distorted face.

"You must know that your scheme has failed."

Again there was that slow smile, as if what Alex was telling him didn't matter.

He'd been caught and was now in police custody. His scheme had failed. Or had it? And I suddenly knew the reason he was smiling.

Redstone. He was still out there somewhere in the rabbit's warren of offices meeting rooms, and passages in Westminster Hall. The question was— what was the rest of it?

"I have no hesitation shooting you," Alex then told Soropkin.

"And deny your people the satisfaction of seeing me hang?" the anarchist viciously replied. "It will never happen!"

"Where is the Prime Minister?" I demanded.

The confidence, the arrogance, the certainty, and that smile...

The sharp report of the revolver was deafening as Alex fired, and Soropkin dropped to the floor, screaming with pain as he clutched his left knee.

I stared at Alex, his expression most serious. He was most certainly full of surprises.

"You won't need that leg to stand up on the gallows," he coolly informed Soropkin as more curses filled the air.

"Or the other knee as well," Alex suggested. "Tell us, where is the Prime Minister?"

As expected, there was no answer. An anarchist to the end, I thought. However, a badly wounded knee would hinder any attempt to escape.

"Where is Redstone?" I then asked. I saw the faint look of surprise in those cold eyes at the realization that we knew a great deal more than he might have hoped.

"It's too late. You will never find him," Soropkin spat between teeth clenched at the pain.

Additional agents had arrived. Alex nodded in recognition. He explained what had happened.

"You need to find the Prime Minister. He's undoubtedly nearby." He paused. "If he's still alive, you need to get him to safety. And Soropkin..." he paused with a glance at the man at the officer's feet.

"He's wounded but make no mistake he is dangerous. He cannot be allowed to escape." His meaning was quite clear.

The hallway outside the office was in chaos as we left the office. A clerk accompanied by the police went door-to-door and announced to Parliament staff that there was an emergency and they were to leave immediately.

They left their offices en masse, some pausing to retrieve a coat or some personal item, then fled down the hallway toward the Central Hall.

We quickly followed and stepped into chaos as those hundreds of members of Parliament, staff, and guests who had returned after the ceremony now made their way toward the main exit and a handful of others that were now manned by the police and more of Sir Avery's people.

Alex held onto my arm or I might have been swept along as people pushed past us. I looked around and finally saw Mr. Conner.

"We have Soropkin," Alex informed him as he pushed his way toward us. "But we were unable to learn anything about Redstone and anything else they have planned."

"Where is Brodie?" I demanded.

Mr. Conner nodded grimly.

"He's gone after Redstone."

## Sixteen

BRODIE LOST sight of Redstone twice, pushed back by members and their staff as the order went out from the Home Secretary that Parliament was to be evacuated.

If he was right about what he suspected Soropkin had planned, there might not be enough time. Deaths would be in the hundreds, the perfect end to the perfect plan of the mastermind of those other attacks.

However, not if he could prevent it.

He pushed his way past those about him desperate to escape and made his way to the last place he had seen Redstone.

His quarry was not there, and Brodie cursed as he grabbed the front of a uniformed clerk.

"What lies in that direction?" he pointed down a hallway, the only way Redstone could have gone.

The young man was startled and stared at him as if he was insane. "The gallery and the House of Lords, sir..." he stammered.

Sir? Not many addressed him as such beyond the MET. He hastily thanked the young man.

Would he be able to find Redstone in time?

In the past, he had not given his own death much thought in consideration of where he came from and his work with the MET. Everyone died, it was just a matter of how and when.

But as he thought of it now, then of her, he wanted to push that back if he could.

Mikaela was strong. She had confronted death at an early age, just as he had. In many ways they were more alike than different.

It was that strength, the intelligence, and perhaps that stubbornness as well that made him want more time with her.

She had accepted him, with his past, the transgressions, and his secrets as far as she knew them. And she was somewhere inside this building with others.

To lose all that now, to one man's insane war against authority, no matter the cost in human lives?

If, as he suspected, something was planned similar to Munich, Paris, and Budapest before that, then time was running out.

He cursed again as he searched the faces of those who fled past him as he made his way toward the House of Lords chamber. Then, he caught a glimpse of Redstone as he shouldered his way past the chamber, down that long hallway. He followed, then lost sight of him again.

When Brodie reached the end of the hallway, he glanced around the corner. The adjoining hallway was short with another door at the end. There was no other place for Redstone to go.

He moved forward with revolver in hand, then stood to the side as he slowly opened that door. A cavernous opening loomed through the darkness along with a dank, musty smell.

His eyes slowly adjusted, and he made out the wrought iron railing at a landing with stairs that descended downward.

He cursed again and stepped out onto the wrought iron landing. There were sounds along with deep shadows, a rumbling sound very much like water, along with the creak and groan found in old places. It reminded him of the Vaults in Edinburgh.

And there were other sounds— human sounds as someone moved something in the passage below, stopped, then came again as if something was being dragged across rock.

He quickly descended those wrought iron steps that spiraled down into the looming shadows, stopped as he reached a slate floor, then heard that scraping sound again. A light flickered at the end of the passage he'd stepped into, then grew stronger as he followed it.

The passage was a rat's nest of pipes some a foot or more across, anchored overhead one on each side of the passage, then running the full length. He heard that rumbling sound again, possibly water from the river that provided water to that massive building above.

There were wires as well, some he recognized similar to wires at the office on the Strand for the telephone, and other tangles of wires no doubt to provide electricity for the chandeliers he'd glimpsed overhead at the Central Hall and the chambers above.

There were new sounds as he approached the end of the passage— a curse, followed by the sound of a hammer, the sound dull against metal as if something was being pried open.

A quick glance about and he was fairly certain that Redstone was alone, foolish for a man who thought himself brilliant enough to bring down Parliament. He stepped into that stronger light.

The scraping sound had been kegs moved about, lined up along the wall of the passage that extended through the passage under the buildings above. The hammering sound had come as Redstone had pried open those kegs, the smell of sulphur thick in the air. Gunpowder!

There were more than a dozen kegs of it, and he realized that there was far more intended with that shipment that had been intercepted. As for the arms discovered with those kegs? He could only guess what the targets might have been.

But with the loss of the shipment Soropkin, Redstone, and others who had joined them, had continued on with the plan to destroy Parliament.

Even as he saw the extent of what they had planned Redstone, unaware that he had been followed, strung wire from one keg to the next down the line with the obvious intention of then lighting the fuse.

Were there others that were part of it? And where was Soropkin?

He held the revolver firm in both hands.

"No further, Redstone."

There was surprise at first on those sharply aristocratic features, then a dark shadow in that hooded gaze.

Too many times he had seen the same in those he had come across in his time with the MET and then private inquiries. From the lowest grifter and thief, to others who tried what Redstone was determined to finish now.

Redstone smiled slowly as he straightened. He was calm, self-assured, arrogant.

"Former Inspector Brodie. Come to arrest me? That is not a complete surprise from one such as yourself, pledged to protect the people of London. But you cannot stop it. Nor can your... wife. Quite a surprise there I will admit. Or perhaps not, given her penchant for those less fortunate than herself..."

"However, this is much larger than yourself... You cannot stop it!

"Or me!"

"Stop!" Brodie told him, one last chance.

"To stand trial and then face the gallows?" Redstone replied. "And give them satisfaction? I think not!"

He came at him, the knife used to pry open those kegs clutched in his fist.

Brodie cursed, then fired. Once, twice, three times.

Redstone fell against him, that arrogant expression now one of surprise as he stared back then slowly slumped to the slate floor of the passage.

"You cannot stop the changes that are coming..." Redstone whispered, a gurgling sound, as blood filled his throat.

Brodie kicked the knife away then crouched down beside Sir James Redstone's body.

"I just did."

## Seventeen

"MISS FORSYTHE, I cannot allow you to remain. You must go where it is safe."

I argued. I threatened. I even pleaded.

It did no good and I was escorted out the main entrance of Westminster Hall, a safe distance away it was explained by an officer with the Met, who failed to be impressed by those arguments, threats, or even my begging which I would never admit to anyone.

"On the Chief Inspector's orders."

In consideration of the MET's reputation for lack of professionalism in the aftermath of more than one scandal that had included the Chief Inspector, I was not pleased.

Police had cordoned off the entire building, moving people back even further, as soldiers appeared. They swarmed inside and then around the entire exterior of the former palace with weapons drawn.

Redstone was dangerous, perhaps more dangerous in some ways than Soropkin. He was titled and wealthy, the epitome of what Soropkin and his followers hated and had vowed to destroy. And then used.

What had changed and persuaded him to become one of them? Was it a worldview changed by what he had seen and experienced on his travels, some which I had shared?

Or perhaps something else had motivated him to join Soropkin's murderous brotherhood?

I thought of something Brodie said after one of our inquiries, when boys, many of whom were orphans who had disappeared from the streets of the East End, had been used for the pleasure sport of others.

I didn't understand it then. How could there be such evil? How could one man who appeared to have everything— wealth and title —become part of an anarchist group that vowed to destroy hundreds of lives?

While another man who came from nothing, had nothing but that office on the Strand and an odd assortment of acquaintances, understood the evil that was there and did everything in his power to stop it?

*"There are some people who are filled with it,"* he had once told me. *"They can never hurt enough, or hate enough. It destroys everything about them, and then destroys them as well."*

I watched now as Soropkin was half-carried, bound and gagged, that horrible gash on his face where the skin peeled back. Then forced into a heavily guarded police van.

There was still no sign of Brodie. And all I could do was watch and wait.

"He will be all right, you know."

I turned at the sound of Alex Sinclair's voice.

"The Agency needs good men."

And I knew that. Brodie was a good man, however not an indestructible one.

What if...?

"You must show me that move you made against Sorop-kin," Alex said as we stood together and continued to watch and wait.

"Most extraordinary!"

He was certainly full of surprises as well. Not that I didn't know what he was doing— a bit of distraction perhaps.

"And you as well," I replied. "You never mentioned that you were proficient with a weapon."

He scooped that shock of hair back from his forehead and smiled somewhat sheepishly, transformed once more into that shy young man who preferred his machines, inventions, and deciphering codes.

"Sir Avery insisted that everyone with the Agency must be prepared to defend themselves," he explained. "He ordered me to the practice yard. It turns out I have quite extraordinary aim."

For which I was grateful. I had another thought. "What about Lucy Penworth? Did Sir Avery's order include her as well?"

"Oh, yes. She is quite fearless with a revolver and reminds me much of yourself."

"You might want to remember that," I told him.

We waited what seemed hours longer, and heard whispered rumors of dozens still inside, barricaded in rooms and offices. If there was an explosion, there would be no safe place for them. I forced back the thought of how many might die.

There was suddenly a buzz of speculation and we saw a stretcher with a blanket pulled over what could only be a body carried out of Westminster Hall, then quickly loaded into yet another police van.

"It's not him," I said quite determined, as if saying it would make it so. "They wouldn't use a police van."

But I knew different. Bodies were collected and then taken to the police morgue or some other facility until the family could be notified.

Family. I supposed that was what Brodie and I were now, the two of us. And Lily was part of it now as well. Where the devil was he?

Alex's hand closed around mine.

"It's not him," he repeated emphatically.

More of Sir Avery's men then appeared, going about the outside of Westminster Hall, then heading the long way around toward the river with more police and soldiers.

There was the sudden sound of shots fired and speculation among those who stood with us quickly followed.

*"What had they found? Who fired those shots? Was it over?"*

Sir Avery's men and the others reappeared, leading several men and a woman between them. A half dozen more police vans rolled forward. Those captured were quickly loaded inside with a great number of mounted police alongside.

"Stay here," Alex told me. "I'll see what I can learn about what has happened."

He set off toward the main entrance of that Gothic hall that loomed up out of the mist with lights ablaze throughout. There was a brief exchange of conversation at the perimeter of the police at the park, then he was allowed to proceed across Whitehall Road.

Far too impatient to wait any longer, I followed. If something had happened to Brodie... if he was injured... I was done with waiting!

"Sorry, miss. No one is allowed past this point," a police officer stopped me.

"I am with Mr. Sinclair. You will let me pass," I insisted. I might as well have been shouting into the wind for the unmovable expression as his face.

"Sorry, miss," he repeated.

I glanced past him to the entrance. I would find a way to slip past the guards there, then...

I pulled the revolver from my bag and marched toward the entrance, then suddenly stopped.

Was that Alex returning already? What had he learned?

My stomach knotted as I looked for that shock of dark hair and a nervous hand as he pushed it back, that shy expression behind those glasses. It was a wonder he hadn't shot himself earlier...

However, the man who walked purposefully across Whitehall Road wore dark clothes, the mist from the river wrapping around him, as Brodie appeared through the crowd that lingered.

"Bloody hell!" I swore and ignored the startled expressions of those nearby as I ran to him. "What took you so long?"

Was that my voice that shook uncontrollably, a mixture of pent-up anger after waiting for hours and some other emotion?

"Business that needed finishin'," he replied in that cryptic, cynical way.

"Is it finished then?" I asked.

That dark gaze met mine. "Aye."

That cold knot in my stomach slowly loosened.

"Sir James?" I then asked.

He nodded and that knot that had tightened at the sight of that stretcher with the body on it finally unwound completely.

There was no remorse, only a vague sadness. How could there be anything else with what Redstone had intended? And then something far more important to me.

"You're not hurt?" I managed to disguise the emotion in my voice. Almost.

"No more than the black eye ye gave me."

I managed a smile. "You did deserve it."

"Verra likely."

That easy familiarity with that sarcasm was there again. I was very glad for both the familiarity and the sarcasm that was so typical at moments like this. And of course, for him.

I once heard something about marital bliss shared by two people. I supposed that this was ours— the end of our inquiry case though not the ending Helen Bennett had hoped for, a plot averted, and several hundred lives saved.

Not a bad day's work, I thought.

"And wot were ye thinkin' ye were goin' to do with this?" Brodie asked as his hand wrapped around the revolver in my hand.

"I thought you might need assistance," I replied.

"With no thought that ye might have been injured, or worse?"

I heard the concern in the words.

"Alex was with me. He has become quite proficient with a weapon," I added, then, "who would have thought?"

"Ye are troublesome baggage, Mikaela Forsythe Brodie."

I leaned into him and slipped my other hand back through that dark hair, my fingers curling into the soft waves.

"I do try," I whispered against his lips.

# Epilogue

EMMA FORTESCUE, *adventuress and world traveler, leaned over the bow of the felucca, one of those small sailboats on the Nile, as it bumped against the wood pier, a body covered with flies pinned between.*

*Her guide, lean, with dark hair that waved over the collar of his shirt, cautioned, "There are many dangers on the river, miss."*

*Perhaps not as dangerous as the heat in that dark gaze fastened on her...*

"Are ye finished then?" another man with dark hair and an equally dark gaze asked as I looked up from my type-writing machine.

It was Brodie of course, who had somehow slipped into Miss Emma Fortescue's next adventure.

"There's just the ending to add and then I will send it off to Mr. Warren," I replied. "He's been most patient in consideration of our last case."

That last case being our inquiry for Helen Bennett in the

matter of the disappearance of her husband, and the Agency's investigation into rumors of a conspiracy against the Crown. The two cases connected in ways we hadn't foreseen and with devastating possibilities had we not exposed and stopped the conspirators.

I added additional lines to that ending page, clattering away at the keys. It was Brodie's suggestion that I bring the machine to the office on the Strand as I spent a great deal of time there. With him out and about on various matters, I had more than enough time to finish my latest novel.

Not that I didn't think of the case, or rather two cases, that we had solved.

We had both called on Helen Bennett afterward. She deserved to know that justice had been served in the matter of her husband's death.

Soropkin had been remanded to Newgate, there to await trial on charges of conspiracy and murder in the deaths of at least two others who had provided information to the Agency, not to mention countless people across Europe in the attacks that had taken place earlier.

However, Brodie speculated that he might not live long enough to be brought to trial. In spite of the horrible crimes committed by others imprisoned at Newgate, it seemed that there was a certain code of justice, if one could call it that.

Among those who were imprisoned for life or condemned to death, where there was most often no loyalty to anyone but self, there was a deep, abiding loyalty to Queen and country. It was very possible that Soropkin would meet another sort of justice there.

Sir James Redstone's part in all of it initially was far more complex and difficult to comprehend.

He had been raised amid wealth and privilege. His family

was one of the oldest, going back generations to the Reformation when an ancestor was presented both title and lands by Henry VIII for his loyalty. No small honor. Not to mention the wealth that went with it.

However, it was discovered that James' father had fallen to drink and gambling and the repercussions that came with it—something I knew a little about.

The vast lands gifted by a king centuries earlier were gone to pay debts. As was the family estate in London in the past year, seized by bankers— and by extension, the Crown.

During very near twenty years of travel to other countries, including those I had shared along with others, he'd nurtured a growing undercurrent of intense dislike toward those he felt had wronged his family.

In addition to the loss of everything that defined who and what Sir James Redstone was and the bitterness that came with it, he found himself drawn more and more to others who had been impoverished and trod upon, cast aside by those they saw as the elite.

With that anger burning inside him, the step into their world and the promise of a new order was a tempting lure. And then with his connections into that world of wealth and privilege, with many unaware of his family misfortunes, he became the proverbial *"wolf in sheep's clothing."*

The perfect plot unfolded to strike at the heart of British power and wealth. Parliament was seen as the heart of power along with those who created the laws. Then, very much like that plot centuries earlier, the decision was made to bring down Parliament and murder the Prime Minister, and the perfect plan was set in motion.

However, not quite perfect...

They hadn't counted on former police inspector Angus

Brodie, who had gone back to the streets and had followed rumors and speculation to Dr. Bennett's secret office.

From that note found among the doctor's papers, it seemed very likely that he had been blackmailed with a threat against Helen Bennett's life, into performing the surgery that allowed Soropkin to move about unsuspected to carry out his part in the plot— the murder of Lord Salisbury.

Of course, there were others who deserved credit as well— Alex Sinclair and that message that was intercepted along with countless people in other countries who remained nameless at the risk to their lives.

Then, there was Lily. Who would have thought that a young girl who was once a maid in a brothel would be able to decipher the code of that message that revealed the plot to strike against Parliament and then assassinate the Prime Minister?

Lord Salisbury had been found alive although somewhat bruised, bound and gagged very near his office. If the plot to blow up Parliament with those explosives Brodie found had succeeded, the end goal of the conspirators would have been complete. He would have died in the explosion along with countless others.

It was all there on the blackboard, my notes complete in the aftermath. I should clean it, I thought, with a look across at Brodie.

There were never any feelings for Redstone, not in the way Brodie had assumed. Perhaps fascination with someone who was widely traveled at the time. It was never anything more, and I had told Brodie as much.

I thought it important to be completely honest, no "ghosts from the past" suddenly reappearing at the doorstep.

The bell on the landing suddenly rang bringing me from

those thoughts. He went to the door, then down the stairs for some message that had arrived.

I had just pulled the last sheet of my manuscript from the machine when he returned. He had opened the envelope and read the note, his expression thoughtful, then a frown.

"From Sir Avery?" I inquired. "I do hope it's not a new inquiry case with the one just concluded."

There was no response. That did not bode well.

I had been hoping that we might find some time away now that we were past the case and the holidays. I looked up.

I have learned to "read" certain things about Brodie in our time together, something he once described as "reading a person," acquired from his time on the street and with the MET. An ability to see beyond the obvious that often led to surprising revelations and clues in the inquiries we have taken on.

A person's body language, their reaction to something said, a look, the sudden shift of the body, the refusal to meet one's direct gaze— all of it quite remarkable in what it might reveal.

There were also those, through a great deal of experience and deception, who were masters at disguising those things. That in itself was often a clue.

What I now saw was a total lack of expression. In the past I had seen just that same reaction, or lack of one on two occasions. Both instances were supposedly to protect me, he said at the time.

"Has something happened?" I asked and thought of my great-aunt at her advanced age, although admittedly she seemed to be defying everyone's expectations for a woman of her advanced years.

Was it something about my sister? Or possibly Lily? That

seemed the more likely given her penchant for rapiers and swords, and escaping her lessons with regularity.

"A matter... I need to attend to." He looked at me then, and for an instant there was the shadow of something there, then it was gone. Or hidden.

A matter he needed to attend to?

There was always something it seemed, new inquiry cases that arrived almost daily, along with his work for the Agency.

However not usually with this sort of reaction, that sudden sense of urgency and the look I had just seen in that dark gaze.

"Should I have Mrs. Ryan plan supper?" I inquired. "Or have it brought from the Public House?"

Not an unusual question since we often worked late at the office. His response was most cryptic.

"No. I have no idea... when I might return."

Which told me absolutely nothing. He then grabbed his coat and umbrella from the coat rack, and left...

# Author Note

The inspiration for A DEADLY DECEPTION came from Egyptian history and an article I read some years ago about advanced medical procedures documented as far back as 1100 BC that included brain surgeries as well as facial reconstruction and the reattachment of limbs.

The central plot then came from the time period of unrest that was spreading across Europe in the late 19th century.

The Agency, as noted before, is a forerunner to that well-known British spy agency, MI6. While that might seem a bit far into the future for Brodie and Mikaela, it's been documented that Queen Victoria had her own spy agency hard at work with all the issues going on in the world.

The London underground, aka the Tube, was first an underground steam railway system that opened in 1863 with limited routes under the city. The first electrified line opened in 1890, and the rest is, as they say, history. The London metro system is considered to be the oldest in the world.

Records regarding gun powder indicate that it was

invented somewhere around the 9th century by Chinese monks mixing different components for new medicine of all things.

European cities had come under attack by anarchists, including a well-planned attack in 1605 by a group of conspirators including Guy Fawkes, a well-known anarchist, when they in fact attempted to blow up Parliament and murder the English King, James I.

The setting at Parliament (Westminster Hall) was a bit of a challenge. That centuries old icon of British law is massive, encompassing nine city blocks along the Thames embankment. The challenge came in describing the enormity of it at the same time using that setting for the conspirators' attack and being able to move Brodie and Mikaela within those walls.

There was previously an enormous fire that gutted a good portion of Parliament in 1834. It was rebuilt in the Gothic style with those upright towers, one at each end that includes that recognizable clock tower, aka Big Ben. It barely escaped the bombings of London during WWII.

As with all old buildings (the original Westminster Hall was the royal residence of several monarchs), it leaks and creaks, and is currently undergoing a multi-year, massive restoration that includes roof repairs, water pipe replacements, new tech systems to carry it into the next century, as well as unraveling and replacing massive amounts of wires, cables, and conduit. Did I already say massive? And far more expensive than the original Westminster Palace.

Fingerprints, morphine, and opium as mentioned in the Deadly series, were in common use in spite of efforts to make narcotics illegal and prevent shipments from the entering the country. They had medical uses but were often, as today, used for other purposes.

Codes in secret messages have been documented as back as

far as clay tablets in Mesopotamia, 500 BC. Ancient Spartans used a transposition cipher to scramble military communications. During both WWI and WWII, coded messages were used by all sides in the conflicts, with messages not only carried by carrier pigeons but deciphered and also delivered by a handful of brave and brilliant women who joined the ranks of spies. But I digress...

Next for Brodie and Mikaela— DEADLY BETRAYAL.

Secrets, murder, and a case that could very well threaten their partnership and that very personal relationship as a woman from Brodie's past returns.

What is the secret she's been keeping? Why is Brodie protecting her? Who wants to silence her? Then, when she is murdered, Brodie becomes the prime suspect and goes into hiding to find the real killer... he claims.

Mikaela must unravel those secrets of Brodie's past. But what will the answers reveal?

She's drawn into a web of lies and betrayal. With assistance from Mr. Cavendish, Munro, and Lily who is quite brilliant and would much rather be chasing down clues than at her lessons. And of course, her great-aunt, Lady Montgomery, and Templeton.

There is also a new partner to contend with— Rupert the hound with that sharp nose, not to mention that he can be extremely fierce and protective.

Look for DEADLY BETRAYAL next in the Deadly Series, coming soon.

Murder is such a dreadful business...

# Also by Carla Simpson

**Angus Brodie and Mikaela Forsythe Murder Mystery**

A Deadly Affair

Deadly Secrets

A Deadly Game

Deadly Illusion

A Deadly Vow

Deadly Obsession

A Deadly Deception

**Merlin Series**

Daughter of Fire

Daughter of the Mist

Daughter of the Light

Shadows of Camelot

Dawn of Camelot

Daughter of Camelot

The Young Dragons, Blood Moon

**Clan Fraser**

Betrayed

Revenge

**Outlaws, Scoundrels & Lawmen**

## About the Author

"I want to write a book... " she said.

"Then do it," he said.

And she did, and received two offers for that first book proposal.

A dozen historical romances later, and a prophecy from a gifted psychic and the Legacy Series was created, expanding to seven additional titles.

Along the way, two film options, and numerous book awards.

*But wait*, there's more a voice whispered, after a trip to Scotland and a visit to the standing stones in the far north, and as old as Stonehenge, sign posts the voice told her, and the Clan Fraser books that have followed that told the beginnings of the clan and the family she was part of...

And now... murder and mystery set against the backdrop of Victorian London in the new Angus Brodie and Mikaela Forsythe series, with an assortment of conspirators and murderers in the brave new world after the Industrial Revolution where terrorists threaten and the world spins closer to war.

When she is not exploring the Darkness of the fantasy world, or pursuing ancestors in ancient Scotland, she lives in the mountains near Yosemite National Park with bears and mountain lions, and plots murder and revenge.

And did I mention fierce, beautiful women and dangerous, handsome men?

They're there, waiting...

Join Carla's Newsletter